Ex Libris

Life on the island
held a fascination

"My congratulations," Craig offered smoothly. "But before you graduate as a true Madeninan, there is something else."

"What?" Hope asked, puzzled.

"This...." Side by side they were very close, their thighs almost brushing. He hardly had to reach to draw her to him with one arm, while tilting her chin with his other hand. Then he kissed her—a long, masterful assertion. Her lips, at first closed and unresponding, soon pulsed in a hungry urgency that shook her to her depths.

She pulled free, feeling her color rise. "If that wasn't taking advantage," she said unevenly, "I don't know what you'd call it."

"I'm afraid I've lost the habit of butterfly pecks," he said stingingly, without the least trace of apology.

Harlequin Premiere Editions

Harlequin
Premiere
Editions

FLASH
OF EMERALD

Jane Arbor

Harlequin Books

TORONTO • LONDON • LOS ANGELES • AMSTERDAM
SYDNEY • HAMBURG • PARIS • STOCKHOLM • ATHENS • TOKYO

Original hardcover edition published in 1977
by Mills & Boon Limited

ISBN 0-373-82108-5

This Harlequin Premiere Editions volume
published October 1981

Printed in U.S.A.

FLASH
OF EMERALD

CHAPTER ONE

As usual, all the way to the office by car, Uncle Lionel had talked yesterday's business with Hope, giving her no chance to discuss with him the letter she had received that morning. But along with her dictation-pad, she took it with her when he rang for her to join him in his room.

After all, Tina was his daughter, which made Tina's present trouble his problem and Aunt Harriet's, more than it was Hope's. In fact, thought Hope, not without irony, it could be said that if it weren't for Aunt Harriet's doting indulgence of Tina, the girl wouldn't be *in* trouble, disillusioned, homesick, and complaining on the 'Nobody Told Me' querulous note of her letter to Hope.

At his desk Uncle Lionel was ready with his correspondence. But Hope forestalled his beginning on it. 'Just a minute, Uncle——' she said.

He looked up, a forefinger flicking impatiently at the papers before him. 'Yes?'

'I've had a letter from Tina.'

'You have? Good. As you know, your aunt was getting anxious, as we haven't heard for some time. How is she? Enjoying herself? Getting on all right with her chief?'

'No,' said Hope flatly.

'No? What do you mean? What can have happened since she first wrote? She was all enthusiasm for the whole West Indian scene then.'

'That was a few days after her arriving in Madenina,' Hope reminded him. 'She hadn't begun her job then. But

now she says the Napier man is mean to her, that he gives
her work she doesn't understand, and expects her to be at
his call all the hours there are. She hates the digs he's
found for her; can't fancy West Indian food, and is having
no fun at all. She wants me to beg you to bring her home
as soon as may be. If not, she threatens she'll run away.
Though where she would run to, on an island the size of
Madenina, is anyone's guess,' Hope concluded practically. 'But she sounds desperate enough to mean it, I'm
afraid.'

'She says all that in the letter?' Lionel Godwin held out
his hand. 'May I see it?' he asked.

'Of course.' Hope passed it over and he read it through.
Then, smoothing it with the side of his fist and pushing
his spectacles up his forehead, he mused, 'I suppose the
truth is we shouldn't have sent her. She was too young.'

'*And* not nearly experienced enough for anyone's personal secretary. So far away too, when she'd never been
abroad, except on holiday to Spain,' suggested Hope.

Her uncle nodded agreement. 'I had my doubts too.
But you know how mad she was to go, and how your
aunt saw it as a wonderful chance for her.'

Hope did know. Also that Uncle Lionel, so shrewd and
forceful in his own business, could rarely say a firm No to
either her aunt or her cousin Tina, and that when they
had both seen Tina's despatch to the French sugar island
of Madenina as a 'wonderful' if undefined chance for her,
he had been less than wise and had agreed to let her go.

He seemed to be thinking aloud now. 'I can't believe
Craig Napier can be as tyrannical as she says. He would
surely make allowances for her, new to the job and her
surroundings, even though I understand he has a bit of a
reputation for being a martinet and a perfectionist. But if

she's as disappointed as she sounds, she's probably making a mess of her work, and he could feel he has a grievance against us for sending her out to him.'

'If he knows she's threatening to quit, yes. But he may not,' said Hope.

'It's a pity,' Lionel pursued his thoughts, 'that I've never met the man—only heard about him on the firm's grapevine. When he was over in the spring and rang us up, he and I were doing a Box and Cox—I was in Barbados while he was in England—and he only spoke to you on the telephone, didn't he, and didn't call in?'

'No. I told him where you were and when you would be back, and asked him if he would care to look in here anyway. But he refused, saying he had barely an hour to call his own as it was.' Hope was remembering a deep, incisive voice and a brief, no-words-wasted conversation. 'And that, as you know, was all we heard of him until he wrote to ask you to engage him an English girl as his personal secretary. Though why he should ask you, you couldn't understand.'

'Nor why he should ask anyone over here, instead of going to an agency. However, we misguidedly sent him Tina, and now what do we do about it?' Lionel appealed.

'Well, if she's determined not to try to make a go of the job, I'd say you have no choice but to bring her home,' Hope advised.

'Letting Napier down? I shouldn't care to do that. Nor, I must admit, to lose face myself with some of the Top Table who thought I was playing favourites when I sent Tina in the first place.'

In the great sugar-importing and distributing combine of Netfold and Islay, of which Lionel Godwin was one of its six branch managers, the Board of Directors was al-

ways known as the Top Table, and though she didn't say
so to her uncle, Hope privately agreed that its members
had shown better judgment than he.

'You did as you thought best at the time,' she told him
loyally, though knowing he had acted on her Aunt Harriet's 'best thinking' rather than his own. She went on, 'If
you ask me now though, you'd be doing worse by Mr
Napier by letting Tina stay on—even if you could make
her, that is.'

'M'm, that's so,' mused Lionel.

'Or——' But there Hope paused for so long that he
looked up at her enquiringly. 'Or what?' he asked.

'Well—I suppose you wouldn't consider sending someone else over to iron things out and to ship Tina home if
necessary? Sending, say, me for instance?' she suggested
tentatively.

'You?' Lionel sounded galvanised by shock. 'My dear
girl, I couldn't spare you! To coin a phrase, you're my
right hand—— And who would take your place?'

Hope smiled at him fondly. He was a dear, really. If
only she had the same rapport with Aunt Harriet! She
said, 'It was only an idea, and of course I've little more
clue to what Mr Napier wants of a secretary than Tina
has. But I *do* know my job, and I do know that Kathy'—
naming her immediate junior in the office—'would jump
at the chance or stepping into my shoes. She's good too.
She could.'

Lionel drew down his spectacles and surveyed her over
them. 'And this idea—it wasn't that you should take on
the job—as a permanency in Tina's place?'

'Oh no, though I might have to play it by ear. Just for
a month or six weeks, perhaps, which should give me
time to train a local girl if Mr Napier would accept one.'

Lionel was musing again. 'M'm, yes. And we can't afford to lose the good will of the Belle Rose plantations——' He lapsed into silence once more, then nodded. 'All right,' he said, and subjected Hope to a long, shrewd look.

'Could be,' he suggested gently, 'that your motive isn't entirely the rescue of Tina? You'd welcome a break? Things haven't been too easy for you lately?'

She looked away, ashamed that he knew. 'Not so very,' she admitted. 'It's probably my fault.'

'Not altogether, I think,' he said. 'But you must make allowances for Harriet. She's missing Tina, and in her view you are no substitute. What's more, you're adult now—twenty-three, aren't you?—and two women in a house, only related by marriage, don't always manage to jell.'

Hope ventured, 'Our friction hasn't only been since Tina left. It's been growing for some time. Yet I've always been terribly grateful to you both for giving me a home after Mum and Dad died, and while I was little, Aunt Harriet was kindness itself.'

'Exactly,' confirmed her uncle. 'Since we're being frank, I'll admit to you that Harriet enjoys power and influence, and this she had over you when you were young. But ever since then she's resented your trying your wings and even your overshadowing Tina a bit, with the resulting flashpoint which at times has had to explode.'

'It's been my place not to let it explode,' Hope said wretchedly.

'My dear, it's not always been possible to avoid it. I've felt the impact myself at second hand!' Lionel comforted her. 'But now we've a temporary solution at least. You'll go out to Madenina and try to bring our silly little girl to her senses, but meanwhile, for goodness' sake, brief young Kathy Tremayne well before you go, for I don't know how I'm going to do without you.'

'You may be saying just that about Kathy by the time I come back,' Hope teased. 'After all, they say no one is indispensable, don't they?'

'Huh! Don't give me that, young woman. Whether or not you are indispensable *I'm* to be left to prove,' growled her uncle. But his smile was kind as he adjusted his spectacles to their rightful place and job, and began to dictate his letters to her.

During eight hours flying and disorientated at thirty-five thousand feet up, Hope had had time for both relief and misgivings.

Relief—at having escaped from Aunt Harriet and the difficulties she had made over Hope's trip, not the least being her ill-concealed conviction that the project had been prompted and engineered through jealousy—Hope's jealousy of Tina who, in her mother's opinion, was only being understandably homesick for a while, and who was far too aware of her good fortune not to settle down to the delights of the Caribbean in time. There was no *need* for Hope to interfere, and as for the Napier man, if he chose to engage a secretary on a kind of blind date, then he deserved what he got!

And misgivings—at all that lay before her. After all, she had little more idea of the conditions awaiting her than Tina had had, though she wasn't carrying with her so rose-tinted an image.

She had asked questions, pored over maps and badgered anyone who could tell her what life on Madenina would be like.

She knew that it was French-owned and governed, and that it lay slightly east of the long rope of islands which curved down from the Strait of Florida almost to the coasts of South America, and her uncle supplied such practical details as that its currency was French, that its people were mixed Creole, American and European, and that its main export was the sugar of which Netfold and Islay took the greater part. But it was Ian Perse, Headquarters' young ambitious Public Relations Officer, who sketched in for her something of the work which would go through the office of the Manager of the Belle Rose estate. Ian had visited Madenina in the course of his work and could report some hearsay about her prospective employer, though he had not met Mr Napier in person.

'You know roughly how he's placed?' Ian had asked. 'That he was managing Belle Rose for Roland de Faye until de Faye was drowned, sailing, and Napier has continued in management for his widow and his small son by his first wife, who was English?'

'Yes, I'd heard something about that,' Hope had said. 'Is Madame de Faye English too?'

'Victoire de Faye? No, she's French and an absentee owner now, one gathers. She seems to prefer Paris to the Caribbean.'

'And Craig Napier? Is he really the monster that Tina claims he is?'

'Perhaps not as bad as she makes out. But he is a bit of a hard character, from all accounts.'

'How "hard"—from a secretary's-eye-view, for instance?'

'I don't know, though his wastage rate in them seems high. Each time I've been over he's had a different one.'

Hope had grimaced. 'Oh dear—bad sign!'

'As you say, bad sign,' Ian had agreed.

That had been their last exchange before she left England, but she was touched when, at the airport, she had been paged to receive a buttonhole of lily-of-the-valley and a Bon Voyage card from him. She had met him first at a Headquarters' Dance and he had asked her to lunch and once to dinner since. That night he had kissed her when he left her, murmuring, 'Nice girl. May we do it again some time?' And Uncle Lionel, who was seeing her off, had approved the posy, saying of Ian, 'Good lad. Going far. Needs encouraging.' But whether by the firm or by Hope he did not make clear.

All day the sky had been a cloudless blue, the sea far below an unruffled expanse. But towards the early tropical evening the aircraft, gradually losing height for landing, had to drop through thickening, rolling cloud. There were lights all over the island, some of them so high as to appear hung from the invisible sky, but the landscape was a blur, and when Hope had gone through Immigration and Customs, rain was falling in a torrential downpour.

Tina, there to meet her, kissed her perfunctorily, asked about the flight, said, 'Nice to see you,' and led the way to a waiting car. Hope, who had been dreading a somewhat hysterical welcome, was relieved but slightly puzzled, especially by the sleek luxury of the car and by the correct deference of the West Indian chauffeur who handed them into it.

As he moved off, Tina indicated the rain. 'It's been doing this more or less every day since I got here,' she grumbled.

'Well, it's November. Not one of the recommended tourist months, I believe,' Hope pointed out.

'Then they should tell you so in the brochures. Silver

sands, gentle zephyrs and sun-drenched days—my foot!'

Hope thought it politic to change the subject. 'Whose car is this? Not Mr Napier's?'

'No. It's Madame de Faye's. She told me to meet you with it.'

'Madame de Faye? I didn't know she would be here! I thought she——'

'Well, she is. She's come back, and she's opening up the Great House—that's what they call the original planter's house on sugar estates,' Tina explained. 'But the Belle Rose one had been closed all the time she's been in France, except for the annexe that's Mr Napier's quarters. He has a daily woman who "does" for him there.'

'Is her young son with her?' Hope asked.

'Stepson? No. He's at school in Europe. He's to come at Christmas, I think.'

'Wasn't it a surprise, her coming back to Madenina?'

'Uh-huh, I suppose so. Though if C.N. knew, he wasn't telling *me*.'

'C.N.? Oh—Craig Napier.' Hope paused, then said heavily, 'We're going to have to talk about him.'

'But not now, for pity's sake. For when I start on him, I can say a lot,' warned Tina sourly.

'So I gather, from all you've written. But all right. Am I staying at the same place as you—with Mrs Paul?'

There was a moment before Tina answered. Then she said, 'Yes. But I'm not taking you straight there now. The Ogre man has ruled that you're to be delivered straight to his office.'

'At this Great House?'

'Oh no. That's only where he lives. To the estate office on the plantation.'

'But at this hour? After flying all day, and before I've

changed or anything!' Hope protested.

Tina compressed her lips. 'From that quarter orders is orders. I tried to tell him you'd be suffering from jet lag, but he just looked through me. And it isn't all that late. It would still be only twilight, if it weren't for the buckets of rain.'

Hope sighed. 'Where are these plantations?'

'Some way out, but nearer to Mrs Paul's than the town. Once they begin, they go on for miles; row upon row of sugar-cane. I've just about *had* sugar, I can tell you.'

'Well, you can soon be free of it now, if you really want to go home,' said Hope. 'You didn't answer Uncle's letter, telling you I was coming out. But that's why he sent me—to tide things over for you until you could go back. I suppose you'll have to give Mr Napier some notice?'

Tina turned her head to look out of the car window. 'I don't want to go home now,' she said indistinctly.

Hope's jaw dropped. 'You *don't*? Why, what's happened? Had a change of heart towards your chief? Or he had one towards you?'

'Neither. He's still quite impossible, but I'm free of him now.' Tina faced about, her wide blue eyes which were the complement of her curly straw-fair hair flashing defiant fire. 'Anyway, now he's got you in my place, why shouldn't I stay on if I want to?'

'Let's get this straight, may we?' Hope urged. 'He hasn't "got" me, except as a fill-gap. I'm still Uncle Lionel's secretary and I'm going back. And how do you propose to stay on, without a salary from Mr Napier? The firm isn't going to be too pleased to allow you to beachcomb out here while your old job is waiting for you in Uncle's office. For instance, how are you going to pay Mrs Paul for your digs?'

'Oh, that!' Tina shrugged. 'But you don't suppose Mum and Dad would grudge my staying on for a bit—at least until I've had a taste of this famous Caribbean weather which I haven't had yet? After being cheated as I have been, I *deserve* a holiday!'

Hope said drily, 'Uncle Lionel could grudge sending me out to rescue you, when you don't seem to need rescuing at all.'

'Though *I* got the impression you were all as much concerned for him as for me?' retorted Tina pertly.

'For Mr Napier? Well, perhaps we were, but——' Hope did not finish as Tina touched her arm and pointed ahead.

'We're nearly there. We're on the estate road now. That light you can see is in the office block, just inside the main gates.'

Hope sat very upright as the car stopped outside a one-storey white wood-cladded building. So much thought about the man Craig Napier; so much speculation; so many words exchanged—what was he really like? Her own pet imagery which ascribed colours to people and things would have described his voice on the telephone as 'dark'. A dark voice, a dark man to match? But as she got out of the car and prepared to meet him, he was only a silhouette in a doorway, light behind him.

Tina introduced him. He came forward, held out his hand. The dark voice Hope remembered said, 'Thank you for making this your first point of call, Miss Redmond. Please come in.'

In his room she looked at him. He *was* dark, tall, informally dressed in patterned silk shirt over slacks. His head was broad at the brow, his deep-tanned skin taut over pronounced cheekbones. One black eyebrow was higher than the other, implying a permanent unspoken question. The eyes which were studying her in return were surprisingly flecked with green.

She had time to wonder what he made of her own looks while Tina was speaking to him. What had he seen? Neither brunette nor true blonde; in-between golden brown, shoulder-length hair; skin with a light powdering of freckles; features in their proper place but without distinction; eyes—well, greyish; lashes which were all her own. Just now, nothing about her at its best, after a day-long journey ...

Tina was asking, 'Do you want me to stay, or shall I wait in the car for Hope?'

Craig Napier looked at her unsmilingly. 'There's not much point in waiting, is there?' he said. 'Have Dickon bring your cousin's luggage, and I'll drive her to Barbara Paul's myself. And as we're only having a business talk, I daresay we can dispense with you as a chaperone.'

Tina's flush showed she was aware of the implied snub. 'Oh, very well,' she said, and went out, closing the door with elaborate care behind her.

Craig Napier looked after her. 'She would love to have slammed it if she dared,' he commented. 'I trust you've grown beyond such infantile defiances, Miss Redmond?'

Hope said, 'If you mean am I older than Tina, I am, by nearly five years. I'm twenty-three.'

'And may I ask whether, as Mr Godwin's confidential secretary, you were consulted, or were a party to our young incompetent's being sent out to me as a personal secretary?'

How to answer that? 'Naturally I wasn't consulted as an equal,' Hope said. 'It was my uncle's decision, and though I admit I questioned whether Tina had enough experience, you hadn't been very explicit about your needs. Until she came out here, Tina didn't realise——'

'Though I'd have thought any London executive circle would know what a personal secretary's duties should be?'

'Yes, well——' This was becoming a somewhat acid exchange, and Hope switched attack. 'I must say none of us understood why you appealed to my uncle at all, when any of several first-class agencies might have served you better,' she remarked, making a challenge of it.

Craig Napier shrugged. 'Sorry to have puzzled you, but this time I decided to try the direct approach.'

'But why to my uncle?' she persisted.

'Because my memory advised me that if he enjoyed the services of super-efficient, no-nonsense young women like the one who had spoken for him when I rang him once, he must have a flair for training them that way. Therefore——' His spread hands finished the explanation.

Hope stared at him. 'That time—*I* answered the phone when you called, and Uncle Lionel was in Barbados!'

'Exactly. Though I didn't get your name.'

'But—but we only talked for a few minutes! Just from that you couldn't have——!'

'All the same, I decided to chance my arm. But look'—with a tilt of the eyebrow—'what I got!'

Hope decided they weren't being fair to Tina in her absence. She said, 'Well, my aunt, Tina's mother, did call your engagement of Tina a kind of blind date, and as she made an equally blind date by coming out to you, one could fairly say that you both deserved what you got. She isn't at all happy with you, Mr Napier.'

He nodded agreement. 'The understatement of the year. She's been cry-baby miserable, and in consequence, as obstructive as a mule. Though not entirely her fault, I suppose, if she came out primed to expect our corner of the Caribbean to rate only just this side of paradise, and its marriage-mart possibilities to be unique.'

Hope flared at that. 'She *didn't* come looking for marriageable men, though when she *is* interested that way she's pretty enough to get any one she wants, I should think. But she did come expecting a better time than she has had, and naturally she's been disappointed.'

'Though she seems in no hurry to shake our dust from her feet. I'd have thought she would have made plans to be off, the minute you came to her rescue. But tell me, how do *you* see your role in this operation, Miss Redmond?'

'Well—to take her place temporarily while you make other arrangements, I suppose. We—that is, my uncle felt he owed you that.'

'And more, I'd say,' was the dry comment. 'But what guarantee have I that you'd be any more competent than your cousin proved to be?'

Hope looked him straight in the eye. 'None, I daresay,' she admitted. 'Except that, within the limits of work that would be strange to me, I think I do know what being a personal secretary entails.'

'I'd hope so. And how long would you be prepared to stay?'

'Well, not indefinitely, of course.'

'But until I decided I could dispense with you?'

She shook her head. 'I couldn't promise that. It wasn't any part of my uncle's plan in sending me out here.'

'No? Yet I can't imagine that you didn't leave him in the hands of a good deputy to you?'

Hope thought of Kathy Tremayne, capable and thrusting for promotion. Kathy could stand in for her ... Aloud she said, 'Perhaps we could shelve the question for a time, Mr Napier? See how I'm able to cope, and go on from there until——?'

He cut in, 'Very well, that suits me. What salary were you getting in London?'

She told him, and he said, 'You'd rate rather higher here, geared as we are to the franc and the American dollar. I'll double that.'

'You're very generous.'

'Only over-generous if you aren't worth it. I'll give you tomorrow to get over your journey, but I'll expect you the next morning. Tina came over from her digs by motor-scooter—they're universal transport here. Can you ride one yourself?'

'Yes, I've had one in England. Can I hire one in the town?'

'Yes, or Tina's should be available, I daresay.' Though she wondered, Hope didn't question why, if Tina were staying on in the island, she wouldn't still need the scooter. She stood up. 'Well, if that's all for now, Mr Napier?' she said, and then was moved to ask a question which, impertinent or not, her curiosity couldn't resist.

'When you applied to my uncle to find you a secretary, do you mind telling me how many others you'd had?' she queried.

Craig Napier didn't answer until he had gathered some papers from his desk, squared them into a pile and brought them with him when he came to open the door for her. Then he said, 'Several. Why do you ask?'

'Because don't you think it might help us both if I knew why they didn't suit you, or you them?'

His silent nod seemed to agree. 'A fair question. So I'd say it was because, though their timing varied, sooner or later all my secretaries deluded themselves either that they were in love with me, or that I was hiding a secret passion for them. And as neither belief contributed to their efficiency or to my tolerance—they had to go.'

The answer was so unexpected that Hope's small laugh came out as a rather silly titter of embarrassment. She said, 'I see. But at least Tina seems to have been an exception to the others.'

'Meaning that she was merely unequal to the job in the first place?'

'Yes. To be frank, I don't think infatuation for you has ever entered her head.'

His hand on the door-handle, he looked up and back. 'Any more, at a guess, than it's likely to enter as level a head as your own? But if you should ever feel the symptoms coming on, do remember, won't you, that you've been warned?' he said as he showed her out.

CHAPTER TWO

THE utter, blatant conceit of the man! Hope took her place beside him in his car, allowing her silence to string out long enough to convey to him her scorn of his implied threat. Then her tone matter-of-fact, she asked, 'How far is it to Mrs Paul's?'

'About three kilometres, and all on the level. Tina could do it on her machine in under ten minutes.'

'And your office hours?'

'Elastic, for you and me, which is something your cousin didn't appreciate. Normally we start early, rarely later than nine. What hours did you keep in London?'

'Nine-thirty to five, or later if I hadn't finished, or if my uncle weren't ready to drive Tina and me home.'

'You lived with him and your aunt, I understand? Why, and since when?'

'For the three years I was going through secretarial college and since. After my father died ten years ago, my mother went back to nursing. She caught a virus from a patient and died from it, and then I went to live with her brother, my uncle, in Richmond.'

The rain had stopped and the clouds were drifting from the lemon-coloured evening sky as a roadside cedarwood bungalow came in sight. 'Barbara Paul's place,' Hope's companion announced as he pulled up, helped her out and unloaded her bags. The garden path to the house was bordered by flowering shrubs, steaming after the rain. The top part of a half-door was open to an interior of

21

which Hope's first impression was of rush mats on a tiled floor, dark furniture gleaming with polish and a french window giving on to a back verandah. Through this window came the slight figure of a woman who stretched a hand to each of them, saying to Hope, 'Welcome to Madenina—I was wondering just when I could expect you,' which struck Hope as odd, since Tina, back before her, would surely have mentioned that she was on her way.

Craig Napier set down Hope's luggage and kissed Mrs Paul lightly on the cheek, while Hope reflected how typical it was of Tina's absorption in her own woes that she had never troubled in her letters home, to describe Mrs Paul for what she was—pretty, young, no accepted 'landlady' type, bright-eyed and with a twist of rich black hair coiled at the nape of her neck. Nor had Tina ever mentioned a connection between her employer and her landlady which would explain the easy intimacy of that kiss.

Meanwhile where was Tina herself? Craig Napier did something towards answering that as he told Mrs Paul, 'I kept Miss Redmond for a briefing and sent Tina back with Dickon.'

'She had the car, then?'

'As I say—complete with chauffeur service.' To the questioning look which Hope sent between them he said, 'Hadn't Tina told you that, since she decided against leaving, she isn't living here with Barbara any more?'

'Not here?' Hope echoed blankly.

'No. She's moved into the Great House, as a guest-cum-employee of Madame de Faye, who has recently come back to the island.' It was Barbara Paul who answered.

Hope said, 'Tina didn't tell me anything about this. And employed—what as?'

'I think the rough idea is that Tina should companion and governess Madame de Faye's small stepson, Crispin, when he comes out from Europe. So you'll be on your own with me. I hope you don't mind?'

'Of course not,' said Hope. 'I'm very grateful to you for putting me up.'

'Fine,' smiled her hostess. 'Now, you'd like to see your room, I daresay.' As she picked up one of Hope's cases, she spoke again to Craig Napier. 'The sun has been over the yardarm for some time. Will you stay for a drink?' she asked.

But he declined. 'No, thanks. I've business in town before I finish. And by the way, I've given Miss Redmond the day off tomorrow. Perhaps you could show her around a bit? Give her the feel of the place?'

'I'll do that,' she promised. 'And another time for that drink, Craig, hm?'

'Twist my arm hard enough——' he quipped, and went out.

Barbara Paul lingered while Hope looked with approval at her small white-furnished bedroom with its tiny window balcony and its mosquito-net draped bed. 'Too bad of Craig not to let you come straight here from the airport to freshen up,' Barbara remarked. 'When was your last meal?'

'That was lunch on the plane.'

'Then, when you're ready, we'll have a drink and then supper. Don't hurry.' At the door on her way out she paused. 'My name is Barbara. Use it, won't you? And yours is—Hope, isn't it? May I call you by it?' she asked.

'Please do,' said Hope, feeling she had made a friend.

The drink was a Creole punch—a light rum with a fruit syrup, ice cubes, topped up with water and a slice of lime balanced on the edge of the tall glass. Supper was a shrimp salad, followed by fresh paw-paw, and when Hope exclaimed at the size of the 'shrimps', declaring them to be outsize prawns, Barbara laughed.

'They're all shrimps to us. Same shape; much of a colour when boiled; some small, some big—why bother with distinctions? You'll find we're a lazy people on the whole,' she said.

'Are you Madenina-born yourself?' asked Hope.

'Born, yes. But my parents are English. They retired and went home after I married.' She paused. 'You'll know about me, I daresay? About how I'm placed? That I'm widowed? Tina will have told you?'

'I'm afraid she didn't,' Hope admitted. 'The one or two letters she wrote home were all of how miserable she was after the first few honeymoon days, and of Mr Napier's brutality to her.'

Barbara grimaced. 'Which I can well believe, as she talked of little else while she was with me. But about myself—and about Nelson, my husband. He was an etymologist, specialising in foreign dialects, and he was on a project, making a dictionary of Caribbean *patois*. Being almost native and speaking it, I was able to help him, and we fell in love and married. But he was only about halfway through the work when he died. He was drowned. Or perhaps you'd heard that?'

Hope shook her head. 'No. How did it happen?'

'Out sailing with Roland de Faye—the owner of the Belle Rose estate, Victoire de Faye's husband, Craig Napier's chief. They were all friends, and often sailed together. But that day Roland and Nelson were alone. It was just about a year ago; our storm season had hung on late, and the boat—it was Roland's—must have caught a squall and broken up completely, for no trace of it, or of them, was ever found.' Barbara paused, biting her lip to stop it quivering. 'That—that was the worst of it—not knowing ... not *knowing*,' she concluded.

'It always is,' murmured Hope compassionately. 'I'm so very, very sorry. But words don't help much, do they?'

'They have to, and one is grateful for them.' Barbara smiled wryly. 'Anyway, Nelson always begged me, if he died first, not to—as he put it—"make a profession" of being a widow, and I've tried not to, with Craig to help me.'

'You are good friends?' Hope questioned, wondering if she could guess what the answer would be.

Barbara nodded. 'Without him, I think I'd have crumpled up and joined my people in England. But Craig persuaded me that I owed it to Nelson to go on with his work, and though I thought it a crazy idea, that's what I've done. And now that dictionary is going to be finished —or else!'

Hope said, meaning it, 'I'm glad, and I think you're wise.'

Smiling, 'Privately, I know I am,' said Barbara. 'The apartment Nelson and I had in town was too expensive to keep on, but while I took a short holiday in England, Craig found me this little place. I can afford it; I've got work to do, and I'm as happy as I could hope to be, without Nelson.'

Hope said, 'I told you I didn't know about the accident. But I mean I didn't know your husband was involved. In fact, I do remember hearing in London that the owner of Belle Rose was dead, and before I came out here now,

someone put me more in the picture—about Madame de
Faye's leaving the island and about Mr Napier's carrying
on in management for her. I was surprised when Tina told
me she'd come back.'

'So were we all,' Barbara confirmed. 'We rather
thought she had left Craig as permanent prince regent, a
role he fills very well, and always has done, even when
Roland de Faye was alive. But that's enough about me
and our affairs. Tell me about yourself?'

Hope told—perhaps more than she would have done
to a less receptive ear than her new friend's. Barbara put
in a quiet question now and then, and one of her last was,
'What about boy-friends? Have you left behind anyone
special?'

Hope shook her head, discarding a brief thought of Ian
Perse and his buttonhole-posy which hadn't weathered
the long flight too well. 'Nobody in particular,' she said.
'I think I need to like people a lot before I go overboard
for them in a romantic way. So if I don't like a man as a
friend, or feel I'm only just another date for him, that's
curtains for me.'

'He wouldn't want to date you, if he didn't like you,'
Barbara pointed out.

'But *really* like me—*as* me, I mean. Not as a scalp to
add to his belt!'

'I know what you mean,' Barbara agreed. 'And I suppose I was lucky—Nelson and I were friends, quite level-
headed platonic ones, before we fell in love and knew we
had it all—liking and love, the lot.' She paused. 'Do you
think you're going to like Craig?'

The question, so irrelevant to their talk of boy-friends
and lovers, took Hope completely aback. *Like* Craig
Napier? Need she? She had only to work for him and do

her best by him in that, hadn't she? And after that flip
warning to her not to like him too much, liking him at all
might prove quite a task! Evading Barbara's direct question, she asked, 'Going to like working for him, you
mean? Well, I suppose I'd better try while I'm here,
though that may not be for long.'

'Not?' Barbara queried. 'I understood you were taking
over from where Tina left off.'

'But not permanently. Only until Mr Napier finds
someone else to suit him.'

Barbara laughed shortly. 'Which could take longer than
you'd think. Craig has a way with men—he practically
never loses an estate hand to any other plantation. But his
secretaries seem to come and go. When he fired the last
one before Tina—an American girl—she told him he
needed a robot, not a flesh-and-blood person with feelings.'

(And from his threat to me, perhaps she had something there, thought Hope). 'What did he say to that?' she
asked.

'I gather he complimented her on the suggestion, and
told her that when robots came on to the agency markets,
he'd be the first in the queue for one.'

'And then he got Tina!'

Barbara agreed, 'As you say, he got Tina. But when he
applied to your chief in London, he hoped to get someone
like you.'

'So he's said to me today, though I didn't quite believe
him.'

'True, I assure you,' Barbara nodded. 'He told me so
himself.'

'Why, how did he describe me?' asked Hope, curious
against her will.

Barbara hesitated. 'Well—can you take this, I wonder? He said you'd sounded on the telephone like a plain jane with her head screwed firmly on——'

'He said more or less the same to my face today,' put in Hope.

'—But that you had a voice that he could bear to hear reciting the telephone directory any time,' finished Barbara.

'Oh——!' said Hope, pleased, though she didn't know why.

The next morning she woke before it was fully light and was surprised to hear Barbara already moving about. They had gone to bed early—Barbara had said that, except on gala nights or after parties, people tended to in the tropics where night and day hours were equal—and evidently they kept early morning hours too.

But after a time all was silent again; Hope fell asleep, and when she got up and dressed a couple of hours later she found Barbara on the verandah with papers and a typewriter on the garden table before her. She hoped she hadn't disturbed her, she told Hope, but she liked to work in the morning hours before breakfast, and when they had had that, they would follow Craig's suggestion and she would show Hope around in her jalopy of a car.

This morning the sky was a clear blue, the air scarcely ruffled by a breeze. They ate on the verandah and Hope had her first fascinated sight of a humming-bird, heard the chatter of tree-frogs, and marvelled that a November sun could possibly be so warm and November flowers so riotously gay.

Over the meal Barbara talked about her work, saying that Creole *patois* derived from both French and English, but as it had no literature and was rarely written, any translation of it had to be by phonetic comparisons with French and English words. It had dropped several letters of the alphabet, had turned the French 'r' into a 'w' sound and was a lazy language, in that it managed without many of the French and English grammatical forms.

'Do you speak it well yourself?' asked Hope.

'Enough to understand it and make myself understood, just as most Madeninans speak English or French, though they use Creole among themselves. When I'm in difficulties with words or constructions—I'm making the dictionary a simple grammar book too—I go to Madeninan friends for help. And Craig is collecting proverbs for my glossary of Creole maxims which are fun and can be very apt,' said Barbara.

'Quote some.'

'Well, if someone is late, what about—"*U deye ko de talo*"—"You are as far behind as two heels"? Or—"*Piti has ka-bat gwo bwa*"—"A little axe can cut big trees"? Not much English to either of them, except "*has*" for axe, but there's a touch of the French "*talon*" in "*talo*", and of *petit* in "*piti*", isn't there?' As she began to clear away the breakfast things, Barbara concluded, 'Nelson used to collect a lot of words and sayings from children. They loved showing off all they knew and he didn't, and I remember the day he and Roland went out for—for the last time, he brought a new one to me which meant—"Good wind; good current; calm sea; let's sail!"—and then he didn't come back.'

'Doesn't it hurt, remembering that?' asked Hope gently.

Barbara nodded. 'Like a knife, sometimes. But I'm going to use it on the title-page of the book—*Bo va*; *bo kuwa*;

lame bel; *navidze*! and I know Nelson would like that.'

'And be proud of your courage, I should think. Then what will you do when the dictionary is finished and published?'

'I'll get a job, I expect. I shall have to, until I see what success it has. Locally, for the tourists and for the schools, it should have some. Further afield, I don't know, but Craig has some influence in England and America, and he could help it along.'

Craig ... Craig. His name appeared almost as a kind of punctuation to much of all that Barbara said, thought Hope. She remembered his kiss of greeting for the other girl; they were evidently close friends—perhaps more?

The place Hope had heard mentioned more than once as 'town' was Port Belain, the island's capital and its port for cruise and merchant ships. The quays were noisy, traffic-choked and hot, but after showing Hope their bustle, Barbara drove into the town down one of several wide boulevards bordered by flowering shrubs and the grounds of luxury hotels.

'They all have their private swimming-pools,' said Barbara. 'They wouldn't catch the tourist trade if they didn't as there are no bathing beaches nearer than about six kilometres north and south. But they're easily reached from Belle Rose; on our way round we'll take some of them in.'

The streets were all French-named, the main ones running straight back from the harbour to the point inland where the finer, tourist-attracting shops began to give place to tawdry markets and cheap cafés and bars, and the good roads and pavements became rutted highways as they climbed the jagged hills which embraced the coastal area in the great curve of their arms.

Barbara and Hope lunched in the town and afterwards they drove along the coast road, coming upon little fishing hamlets where the beaches were draped with drying nets, and crescent coves, some of them 'developed' by the tourist hotels with sun umbrellas and pedalos and snackbars; others more lonely, backed by sprawling tamarisks and with wind-slanted palms and sea-grape trees growing on their untrodden sands almost to the water's edge.

Barbara named some of them for Hope—Witch Creek, Cove of Desire, Cloud's Nest Bay—and told her how to reach them from Belle Rose without needing to touch the town.

Though beyond the gentle lap-lap of the lazy surf the sea looked like green silk, the girls hadn't come prepared to swim, and at about fifteen kilometres out they turned back along the coast road again. On the promenade fronting one of the holiday hotels they had passed earlier, Barbara had to halt the car in traffic, and as they waited she pointed out a car parked with others at the balustrading above the beach. In the driving-seat sat a man, upright and immobile, whom Hope recognised.

'That's Madame de Faye's chauffeur, isn't it?' she asked.

'Yes. Dickon,' Barbara confirmed. 'Looks as if Victoire may have come to the beach. If so, perhaps it's a chance for you to meet her. I'll park.'

She edged the small car into a space and they went over to the big one. 'Madame is at the beach?' she asked Dickon, but he shook his head.

'Not Madame. I bring Missus Godwin. She just gone down to the beach 'long away——' He pointed, and following the direction of his finger Hope saw Tina in a white bikini, threading her way between prone sun-bronzed bodies towards the sea. Barbara called to her over the balustrade; she stopped, turned and beckoned, waiting for them to join her.

'Luxury for some. You get chauffeured even to the beach,' commented Barbara.

'Yes, but only until Madame gets a little car for me to drive—so that I can take Crispin around when he comes out. Then I'll be independent. Where are you going or have been?' asked Tina.

'On a tour, to show Hope the geography, and when we saw the car and Dickon, I thought it might be Victoire here, not you, and I brought Hope to be introduced.'

'Oh. What's the hurry?' Tina sat down and began to oil her arms and legs.

'No hurry. Just being polite, that's all.'

'Well, bring her up to the Great House when I go back. But I'm going to swim first. Are you going to, too?'

'No, we didn't bring any gear. And anyway, I prefer somewhere quieter, like Cloud's Nest or Desire——' Barbara broke off and looked at her watch. 'Besides, I ought to get back. I've got a woman coming to see about doing for me on one morning a week. So look—if I left Hope with you, and you took her to meet Victoire, could Dickon drive her back afterwards, do you think?'

'Sure,' said Tina. 'But I'm going to have my swim first.'

Revelling in the glorious warmth of the sun, Hope lay down beside her, making a pillow of her head with her crossed arms. 'Even if it does rain a lot, if you get sun like this in between, I don't know what you have to grouse about,' she said.

'Forgetting, of course, that even when the sun did shine, a wretched wage-slave like me didn't often get the chance to enjoy it. It's always seemed to be raining whenever I got off that sadist's hook.' Tina paused. 'Notice, did you, how smoothly Barbara got out of bringing you up to the House to meet Madame de Faye?'

' "Got out of"? It was she who suggested introducing us, when she thought Madame was here,' Hope objected.

'Sense of duty. Or to get it over with, without having to accept any hospitality.'

'What makes you say that?'

'They don't get on.'

'Not? Why not?'

Barbara shrugged and got to her feet. 'Reasons,' she said cryptically. 'I'm going to swim now. Shan't be long.'

Half an hour later she was willing to return to the car, and on the drive Hope took her to task for letting her suppose they were both to stay with Barbara for as long as she, Tina, was on the island.

'Yes, well, I didn't tell you I *was* still there,' said Tina sulkily.

'Nor that you weren't,' Hope retorted. 'What's more, I had to hear from Mr Napier and from Barbara where you were and what were your plans. Anyway, what makes you fancy yourself as a governess to a boy of nine? You don't know anything about children, and you've certainly never had to teach one.'

'So what? I should hope I can keep ahead of a nine-year-old in arithmetic and reading. Besides, teaching him isn't really the idea. It's to keep him off Madame de Faye's hands as much as anything.'

'Just while he's on holiday? I'd have thought she would want to see as much of him as she can before he has to go back.'

'Though he may not be going back to Europe. I don't know. I haven't been told,' said Tina.

Dickon turned in off the road up a drive which led to a house built in a very different style from the modern hotels and villas Hope had seen during the day. This mansion was not unlike a French château of the eighteenth century, with a long façade of deep windows, the frontage shadowed by a pillared portico the full length of the building. The walls were gleaming white, the roof of mellowed apricot tiling. Oleanders and cacti in big tubs flanked the main doorway. Window-shutters laid back against the walls enhanced the French design.

'The Great House? It's lovely,' Hope commented.

'Reminds me of something out of *Gone With the Wind*,' said Tina as they alighted and Dickon drove the car on to the side of the house and through a high *porte-cochère* into what was probably a courtyard. 'Craig Napier has his quarters through there,' Tina indicated. 'They're an extension of the stabling. That's his car under the wall. Looks as if he's at home.'

She led the way into a marble-paved hall, divided from an inner hall by decorative wrought-iron trellis. A door stood open to a drawing-room. They crossed this and went through a french window to a terrace where a woman, presumably the lady of the house, lay on a cane sunlounger.

Her brief playdress of white sharkskin had a pleated skirt and a halter-top, knotted at the waist and on each bare shoulder. She was slim and long-legged; her rich auburn hair was piled on her head in a studiedly careless bunch. She did not rise as the girls approached, but merely removed her dark sunglasses and surveyed Hope appraisingly. To Tina she said in English with a trace of accent, 'You are back? And this—is your cousin? You hadn't said you were meeting her?'

'I wasn't. Craig'—Hope noted Tina's use of his first name here— 'gave her the first day off, and Barbara drove her round to show her the island. They hailed me at Moule, and I brought her to meet you. Hope—Madame de Faye, my hostess. Of course I have told her about you,' Tina concluded.

Hope took the hand offered by Victoire de Faye. 'Welcome to Madenina,' the latter said mechanically, and to Tina, 'and Barbara Paul? Did she come up too?'

'No. She had an engagement at home——'

'Ah——' The corner of Victoire's mouth lifted in the ghost of a smile.

'So I took the liberty of saying that Dickon would drive Hope back. Was that all right?' asked Tina.

'Of course. Sit down, won't you, Miss Redmond? Or may we call you Hope, as we call Christine Tina? Tina—chairs!' The last two words were a crisp command which Tina obeyed with alacrity.

They talked as acquaintances, Madame asking about Hope's flight out and her opinion of such of Madenina as she had seen, and Hope admired the beauty of the house, saying she hadn't expected such elegance. Craig Napier and Tina's broken relationship with him was not mentioned; nor was her prospective employment as the boy Crispin's 'governess'. But, as in the matter of the chairs, Hope thought there was more than a hint of an employer's tone in the way Madame said after a while, 'Tina, the flowers in the salon are half-dead. You'd better get some more before evening—or now, perhaps. Put them in the garden-room and I'll arrange them when it's cooler. But not hibiscus—I have *told* you that it doesn't last twenty-four hours, have I not?'

'Yes,' said Tina, rising.

'And you could show your cousin the gardens, if she cares to see them. I shall be going to change presently.'

It was a subtle dismissal and Hope took it as such. As she went with Tina her imagination was dressing Victoire de Faye exotically—in evening gowns and furs, and arranging that great swathe of hair into coils and coronets— and acknowledged that Tina's hostess was a great beauty.

Aloud to Tina she turned this thought into the understatement of, 'Madame is certainly a looker, isn't she? And too young for a widow—I shouldn't think she's thirty.'

'Nothing like, I'd say,' agreed Tina.

Hope was thinking again. 'What do you suppose she meant when, after she'd asked me if I should be comfortable at Barbara Paul's, she said, in a meaning sort of way, "And of course it is *rather* important for Barbara to have someone there with her—as Tina was, and now you"?'

Tina did not reply. She only smiled.

'Well?' urged Hope.

'Well, see yourself as a chaperone, can you? I admit I found it a giggle when Madame suggested that I was one.'

'A chaperone for Barbara Paul? Why should she need one?'

'For the usual reason, I suppose—to keep people from talking. Seems, as far as Madame hinted, that when Barbara and her husband lived in town, Craig Napier spent a lot of time at their apartment. Too much time. So that when he moved Barbara out to that cottage it was supposed she was his *petite amie*, and they could keep their rendezvous out of the public eye.'

'How perfectly beastly of people!' exclaimed Hope.

'It's not an uncommon thing for men to do,' Tina shrugged.

'But only when they're running a clandestine affair, and there's no need. Barbara Paul is a widow.'

'Well, perhaps Craig prefers things the way they are, and as chaperones, when he or she realised people were talking, you and I were heaven-sent.'

'You don't *know* the way things are!'

'Neither can you,' Tina capped. 'But on the evidence—well, didn't they kiss when he drove you there last night? And you'll have noticed that he couldn't wait to get rid of me and Dickon?'

'Yes, but——' Hope switched her attack. 'Anyway, I'm surprised Madame de Faye discussed her manager's private affairs with *you*, as his secretary.'

'Oh, she didn't, while he employed me. And she hasn't "discussed" him since—only dropped hints and made it fairly obvious she doesn't like Barbara Paul.'

'Doesn't she like Mr Napier either?'

Tina pursed her lips. 'Difficult to say. She must know she couldn't afford to lose him as her estate manager; I'd say they have a kind of love-hate relationship, and you know where *that* sometimes leads.'

'Why, where does it lead?' countered Hope, not wanting to agree.

'According to the novelists, wherever the stronger one wants it to lead,' was Tina's sententious reply as she reached for some high-blooming yellow allamanda blossoms and added them to the mass of colour in her trug.

When they returned to the house the sun had gone from the terrace and Victoire de Faye had moved back into the salon. Craig Napier was with her. Though he rose when the two girls came in, they went on talking.

Victoire was saying, 'And you are insisting that I leave it to you?'

'As you've surely understood all along that you must.'
he retorted coolly.

She did not move, but somehow conveyed the air of
turning on him. 'Then why bring to me at all?' she
demanded on an acid note.

He sketched an ironic bow. 'For the courtesy of consulting you,' he said.

'Euh!' The sound was one of disgust, and in the silence
which followed Hope apologised for having to leave and
waited for her hostess to tell Tina to summon the chauffeur. But it was Craig who offered. 'I'll drive you,' he said.
'I have to go back to the office.'

'Thank you.' Hope was uncomfortably aware of Tina's
knowing wink and thinking she could read it aright as
saying, 'What did I tell you? Any excuse to get out to
Barbara Paul's cottage, even on the prosy errand of taking you home!' Tina had won that round.

On the drive Craig Napier showed no curiosity as to
how Hope had spent her day, but suddenly without preliminary questioned, 'Before you left London, were you
briefed as to my precise authority with regard to Belle
Rose?'

Not understanding the purpose of the question, 'I think
I understand it, yes,' she told him. 'That you're Madame
de Faye's estate manager—isn't that right? And why do
you ask?'

'Because I think it necessary that, as my confidential
secretary, you should appreciate quite clearly just where I
stand in the matter of executive decisions about the estate. For instance—the discussion of which you happened
to hear the upshot just now. It had been on the question of
a proposed merger with a minor sugar estate—the Friole
—which in my opinion could show no advantage what-

ever for Belle Rose, though Victoire de Faye tends to favour it. And in my making it clear that the decision, when it comes, must be solely mine, it seemed to me that you may have thought that I was unnecessarily pulling rank. Did you?'

Hope queried, 'You mean—overriding Madame de Faye about it? But how could I judge, from the little I heard? And would it matter if I had thought so, anyway?'

'Matter?' he took her up sharply. 'Your opinion *matter*? Of course not. The reason I asked was because I needed to be quite clear that you understand exactly that in any decision regarding the estate, my word goes. Finally. And assuming the full support of my staff—which includes you. You in particular, as the *aide* nearest to me. *Do* you understand that?'

Hope said quietly, 'I think so. In fact, you can rest assured I've never doubted your right, as manager, to arrogate to yourself all the authority you need. Though I must say——' She checked. 'But you aren't interested in my opinion, are you?'

He shrugged. 'As long as we're clear on the major issue, I daresay I can bear to hear it. Well?'

'Just that I'd have thought you owed the owner of Belle Rose rather more than the mere courtesy of being consulted, that's all.'

He nodded. 'As I thought. As well then, isn't it, that I decided to pinch the possible small canker of disloyalty in the bud?'

Hope had to bite back a sharp retort. 'If you thought it necessary to warn me as to whose side I'm on in any dispute—just as well,' she agreed.

But ironic as she had tried to make her tone, seemingly it did not register with him. He said briskly, 'Good. As

long as you recognise that, whatever my personal relationship to Victoire de Faye, I am the final arbiter in anything concerning the estate, and you, with all the other
people I employ, are four-square behind me.'

At which piece of cool dictatorship Hope could not resist a murmured, 'And surely no despot could ask more?'
—only to hear him laugh outright, as if in genuine
amusement.

'You show a pretty line in repartee,' he said. 'But don't
be too sure, will you, that I can't sometimes match it?'
And then from amusement at her expense to the practical,
'Anyway, to work tomorrow. I'll expect you at the office
at half-past eight.'

At the bungalow he switched off the engine and went in
with her, meeting Barbara almost on the threshold, as
had happened the previous night.

They kissed. Barbara said, 'Craig! Why, how nice!'

He said easily, 'If that drink is still on offer, I'll take it
now if I may.'

'Of course,' she smiled.

'I'll get them,' he offered. 'What are you having? And
you?' he asked Hope.

It seemed to her, as she told him and as she saw his
familiarity with Barbara's drinks cabinet. That Tina had
also won round two.

CHAPTER THREE

HOPE took care to be punctual the next morning, but the evidence of Craig Napier's parked car showed that he was at his office before her. When she had ridden in through the gates she had joined a group of West Indian girls, also on mopeds and bicycles, and when she dismounted, one of them, who said she was a junior clerk, showed her where to wheel her machine alongside others in an open-sided shed.

Hope went in by the door she had been taken to on the night of her arrival. The other girls had used another one. Craig Napier was already at his desk. He looked up briefly and half-rose as Hope entered, then spoke to her, having seemingly returned most of his attention to the papers before him.

'You managed the ride over all right?'

'Yes, thank you, and one of your staff showed me where to park. She spoke to me in English,' Hope added.

'She would, having heard you're Tina's cousin. Most Madeninans are bi-lingual in French and English, though they may use the *patois* among themselves.' Continuing to sign sheets and flip them from him, he went on, 'Normally you will work in here with me, and absent yourself when I tell you to.' With a nod, 'That's your desk over there. If you'll settle yourself in, I'll attend to you in a few minutes.' Another nod indicated an inner door. 'Your cloakroom, and a cubbyhole with a chair and a desk, to which you can adjourn when I don't want you here.'

The view from her desk, facing a window, was of a scene which the premature darkness had hidden from Hope the other night. In the mass it was a sea of green on a far-stretching plain; viewed more particularly, the 'sea' was rank upon ordered rank of sturdy, heavily fronded shoulder-high plants—the all-prevalent sugar-cane which was the island's business and was to be hers for as long as she stayed in Madenina.

She had stepped to the window to look out at it and did not hear her chief's approach until he was close behind her. Echoing her thoughts, he said, 'Well, there it is—our be-all and end-all, and the stuff that shows up at home as coloured coffee-crystals and blankets for Christmas cakes —not to mention Demon Rum. Is it much as you imagined it, or have you seen it growing before?'

She shook her head. 'Only in photographs. There's a series of them in the boardroom in London. And does it go on and on—endlessly like that, all over the estate?'

'Oh no. At this eye-level it may look so. But it's broken up between each plantation by roads for vehicles—some horse and mule-drawn, some motorised—for bringing up fertilisers and shipping the cut cane to the processing-plants. See from here'—his hand familiarly at her shoulder and his finger guiding her glance—'there's a truck moving through there on the right. The road is one of the limits of this nearest plantation; you can't see as far as the boundaries of the next.'

'And what's happening now?' she asked, as much as to hide her awareness of the unnecessary tightening of the pressure on her shoulder, as to show her interest. Once he had gained her attention for what he wanted to point out, she would have expected his hand to drop indifferently away. And even when it did as she turned to face him, he did not step back, but remained close, rocking back on his heels, his eyes intent upon her. For the moment there was an ease to his manner which she could reconcile neither with Tina's view of him as an ogre, nor to her own conception of him as an aloof employer with somewhat inflated ideas of his magnetic effect upon his female employers.

No wonder, she thought fleetingly, that those impressionable girls he claimed to despise should have warmed too much to such occasional camaraderie which they didn't expect from him and of which they hoped disproportionately. Almost she was in danger of melting to it herself ...

He answered her question. 'This and that. We're about through with our big *ratoon*. Come New Year, we'll be working up to our next in March or April. We cut twice a year, with the autumn *ratoon* the more important.'

'*Ratoon*?' Hope queried.

'Crop. Harvest. Cutting. *Ratoon* is a more or less universal sugar word.'

'And do the canes yield again, once they're been cut?'

'For several seasons more if they don't fall victim to disease. Deteriorating gradually, of course, when they're replaced by cuttings from youngish canes.'

'How are they processed for the sugar?'

'By crushing. The solid content is sugar; the liquid comes down as molasses, the best quality of which goes for rum. You'll know of course that the sugar is shipped in its raw state, for refining in the importing countries?'

Hope said, 'Yes, I know that end of it. It was this end I only knew in rather vague theory.'

'Well, you'll witness the whole cycle here.'

The whole cycle? How long did he suppose she was prepared to stay? Hope wondered as he went on, 'You show a refreshing interest, I must say. Usually I've had to make a continuous lecture of my briefing. But you ask intelligent questions, and it makes a pleasant change.'

As he spoke he had left her to return to his desk, and she went over to hers. 'Thank you,' she said. (What did he expect of a 'plain jane with her head screwed on' than that she should want to know something about the raw material of her job?) Deciding to risk a snub if she put a more personal question, she asked, 'Have you always worked in sugar yourself?'

He nodded. 'I did a year of research after I took my science degree, and then came out here. Roland de Faye's father was the owner of Belle Rose then, and Roland and I worked up from the ground floor together, so to speak. Roland had married for the first time before he inherited, when he offered me the managership. His wife, Irene, died when their boy Crispin was five. He and Victoire were married only a couple of years when he was drowned. Meanwhile, I carry on for Victoire.' He paused. 'Anything else that you feel might put you in the picture?'

Hope thought, then said, 'Only something which concerns myself. I know you said my hours must be elastic, but what free time might I normally expect?'

'Hadn't Tina told you?' he questioned. 'You should be free from about noon on Saturdays through Sundays. We break at half-noon every day—in theory—and there's a canteen. Back again at three, when we work until sundown—around seven or so. And if that interferes with your evening leisure, as Tina claimed it did with hers, then I'm sorry. It's the custom of the country, and you must conform.'

'I see,' said Hope calmly. 'That sounds generous, and in that long lunch-time, I suppose I could go back to Mrs Paul's?'

His reaction to that suggestion was so swift and decided that she was startled. 'I shouldn't plan that as a regular thing,' he advised. 'Barbara Paul likes to have a session of work before breakfast——'

'Yes, I know,' put in Hope.

'Starting again after she's done her morning chores, and I don't think she would welcome the interruption of getting a meal for you.'

'I'm sorry, I didn't think. I'll eat at the canteen,' said Hope. She hadn't asked Tina what her routine had been, but if her chief had put a similar veto on her midday habits, she thought she could guess what Tina's petty cynicism would have read into it—that quite possibly he visited the cottage himself at that hour——

Hope started, and knew she had quite visibly shaken her head, in rejection of the suspicion that the thought had crossed *her* mind too. She glanced over at Craig Napier. But evidently he hadn't noticed that involuntary movement of her head, for his next remark was detached, businesslike. 'Well, if that's all, I'll put you to work. What filing systems do you understand?' he said.

She was occupied that morning with compiling pay-slips. The plantation hands were paid by piece-work, so that each pay-slip was different and had to be checked with the hourly rate for the job. Once he had explained the system to her, Craig Napier left her to it. He went out and returned to the office several times, taking no more notice of her than if her desk had been unoccupied, and

leaving Hope to wonder if Tina, used to the easy camaraderie of the London office, had seen his treating his
secretary as a mere adjunct to his own job as one of his
major brutalities. And those several others who, he
claimed, had hoped for a warmer relationship with him—
had they too had to make do with the occasional word of
praise tossed their way? As she herself had been encouraged by his dry appreciation of her interest and by
the hearsay of his having told Barbara that she had a
pleasant voice? Encouraged, but not bowled over, by any
means. Just—pleased. No more than that . . .

He was still at his desk at noon when she went to the
self-service canteen, and his car was again outside when
she returned at three o'clock after getting acquainted with
some of the other clerks and listening to their volatile
French chatter which she wished she were going to have
time to understand.

They were dressed so gaily too—in reds and yellows,
flirting dirndl skirts and wearing cheeky topknots in
their black hair. When some of them wheeled off to their
homes they looked like a flight of exotic birds and made
as much concerted noise as so many starlings. Watching
them and revelling in the sunshine, Hope thought of how,
at this season, she and Tina would have gone in winter
boots and wrapped in topcoats to their lunch, and marvelled that Tina could possibly have allowed Craig
Napier to spoil this idyllic place for her.

Back in the office Hope finished the pay-slips and told
her chief so.

'Then take them down to Winston Fortune, the pay-
clerk, in the *boucan*—that's the pay-office at the other
end of the building. Tell him to check the total and go to

the bank for the cash. That's Thursday routine, of course, but he won't be expecting to see you.'

'Does Mr—er—Fortune speak English?' Hope hesitated.

Craig Napier laughed dryly. 'What do you suppose—with a name like Winston? British to his grass-roots, he claims—though he's never travelled farther than to Barbados on our island-hopping plane. He'll welcome you as he would a long-lost sister; as he did Tina, who made it clear she was Not Amused and lost a lot of his respect in consequence.'

When Hope came back she was laughing. 'Mr Fortune was quite wistful about the Royal Family,' she said. 'When he heard I lived in London, he wouldn't accept that I hadn't the chance to see one of them at least every day.'

'Yes, that's his cult—he knows all their intricate relationships, right back to the Georges,' Craig agreed. He stood up. 'I have to see some of the foremen on the plantation now. If you'll come along, you can get some idea of the layout of the estate. You'll need to know it.'

They went in his car. As he drove he made informative conversation. '*Boucan* is interesting,' he said. 'It's the old Carib name for an open fire where the *boucaniers*—French refugees from the Spaniards—used to gather for a common meal of spit-roasted meat. The *boucan* became a central point of business in the sugar trade, and for an estate office the name still holds.'

He described for Hope the work that was going on—the weeding by women as well as men, the clearing of trash after the autumn crop, the traffic in fertilisers for the spring crop to come. He made a detour to show her the workers' living quarters—neat one-storey cottages, part-owned with pride by their occupiers. Belle Rose, he told Hope, had been the first of the Madenina estates to get rid of the shanty-town image. That had been Roland de Faye's ambition, and he, Craig said, counted himself privileged to have seen the project through.

There were long intervals during which Hope waited in the car while he waylaid various men and sometimes walked away with them, still talking. It was evening before he drove back to the office, when he told her she could call it a day and offered to drive her home.

She demurred, 'I have the scooter, and I shall need it for coming to work in the morning. Besides, I've only done one journey on it, and I must get used to it.'

'Very well,' he said indifferently, and let her go to the bicycle shed which was empty of all the machines but her own, showing she was the last of the girl-clerks to leave. She had only been on her way for a very few minutes when, with astonishing force, and out of an apparently almost clear sky, the rain came down. Clouds piled swiftly; the downpour worsened; the rutted road, already studded with half-filled pools from previous rains, became a quagmire, and after a plunge into and out of one of the potholes, the scooter's engine gave a couple of warning splutters and died.

'Water in the plug,' Hope diagnosed, giving the starter an optimistic kick. No response. Another kick, with the same result. She dismounted, debating whether to deal with the plug or, as she hadn't much farther to go, to walk on and push the machine. Doing either, she was going to get soaked through, but had just decided to walk when a car—the one in which she had spent the afternoon—overtook her and stopped.

Craig Napier got out of it, opened up its back, took the

scooter from her grasp and heaved its weight aboard.
'That'll teach you to trust the weather of a whole
Madeninan day,' he said. 'Get in.'

She obeyed, wiping rain from her hair, her face and her
bare arms with a handkerchief which became a mop-wet
rag. When he joined her he offered her his own. 'How
could I know it was going to rain out of *that* sky, and before I'd gone much more than half a kilometre?' she
complained.

'You couldn't, but you'll learn,' he said unsympathetic-
cally. 'Anyway, how do you suppose we grow crops as
lush as sugar if we don't have rain and plenty of it?'

She wondered why, if he were on his own way home,
he had followed her up; the Great House and his quarters
were in quite a different direction. When he had offered to
drive her, had he intended all along to drive to Barbara
Paul's, and so hadn't cared whether she accepted a lift
there or not? If it hadn't rained, would he have sketched a
salute to her when he passed her and have already been
with Barbara when she did arrive? She frowned, an-
noyed with herself for following Tina's speculations for
the second time that day. Craig's *petite amie*, Tina had
called Barbara, making an ugly slur out of the simplicity
of 'little friend' and implying, without saying as much,
that the bungalow was their love-nest. And here was she,
Hope thought with distaste, actually wondering too. And
she would not—would *not*! From here out she was forgetting it. She didn't want to know.

Her surmise had been wrong. At the bungalow he
stayed only long enough to let her get out and to push her
scooter into the lean-to which was its garage. He did not
wait to see Barbara, who clucked concern at Hope's wet
state and sent her to take a hot bath. The evening cleared

out after the storm, enabling them to sit out on the verandah until it was quite dark.

Barbara asked what Hope expected to do in her spare
time, and Hope countered by asking what social life there
was; what, for instance, Tina had found to do.

Barbara grimaced. 'Not much, I'm afraid. That was one
of her grouses—that she didn't get to know anyone but
me. But as she seemed to think she would lose caste if she
appeared anywhere without a male escort, she never
reached first base in meeting anyone. She has her car, by
the way,' Barbara added. 'She drove over in it at lunch-
time, expecting to show it off to you.'

'I didn't come back. I lunched in the canteen. Mr
Napier said you worked through once you started, and
wouldn't want to be interrupted,' said Hope.

'Do call him Craig. I'm sure he'll call you by your first
name except when he wants to be very formal in the
office,' Barbara suggested gently, 'and though that's true
—that I do work on through the afternoon, I hope you'll
feel free to come back any time you want to. Though if I
were you, I'd keep some swimming gear over there. Between noon and three you'd have plenty of time to scuttle
over to Cloud's Nest for a dip, especially if I gave you a
packed lunch to take with you.'

'Thanks awfully. I'll do that sometimes,' Hope agreed,
relieved that another of her surmises about Craig and
Barbara had proved wrong, since Barbara obviously had
nothing to hide as to how she spent the midday hours. She
had been at home to Tina this morning; she would welcome Hope 'any time', she had said. Hope reminded herself to snub Tina with facts when they next met.

Barbara was saying, 'There's the Planters' Club. It's for
the owners and managers, of course. But every fortnight

they have a Ladies' Night—the next one, this Saturday, the day after tomorrow. You'll meet people there. Would you like to go? With me, I mean?'

Hope said, 'I'd love to. But if you're going, won't Mr— Craig be taking you?'

Barbara looked away. 'Oh, Craig and I are friends, but we don't go about together. Anyway, if Victoire de Faye is going to the Club on Saturday, he'll be escorting her. But I wonder if Tina might change her mind and come with us, as you'll be going. Shall I telephone the House and ask her?'

Hope listened to the one-sided conversation, heard Barbara say, 'Oh, all right. Nice for you,' and when Barbara hung up she reported that Tina was going to the Club, but with Luke Donat, the son of another planter, to whom Victoire de Faye had introduced her.

'She implied that it hadn't taken her long to make some social contacts, once she got out of Craig's and my clutches,' laughed Barbara without a trace of rancour.

'What goes on at the Club, and what does one wear?' Hope asked.

'People meet and chat; a lot of sugar "shop" is talked,' said Barbara. 'There are buffet refreshments and some dancing and card-playing. The men dress informally; the women like to wear long. Anything pretty you have with you will do.'

The Planters' Club building was on the quays of Port Belain, its next-door neighbour the Yacht Club, both overlooking the latter's marina. The foyer and the big room beyond it were crowded with people, drinking and talking in groups. Everyone seemed to know everyone, and it was not long before Barbara and Hope were drawn into

a group where the introductions were made mostly by
first names, as if it didn't matter who was who, as long as
they were good company.

As she listened to talk in which she wasn't joining,
Hope looked about her. Tina was there, looking at her
butterfly prettiest. Her companion was a darkly hand-
some youth, who moved with slim-hipped grace when he
put a possessive hand under Tina's elbow and led her towards another group where Victoire de Faye, at the centre
of a ring of men, was holding court, Craig Napier beside
her.

Presently the crowds broke up and drifted off to different purposes. The bar was an attraction. So were the card
tables. The shift of population cleared the floor of the big
room, and dancing began to a three-piece band playing
Latin-American and calypso rhythms. Victoire de Faye
did not dance. Craig had left her to join some men at the
bar, but she never seemed to lack company, one man suc-
ceeding another in seeking her out. From the bar Craig
went to ask Barbara to dance at the same time as Hope
was being partnered by a young West Indian from An-
tigua, whom Barbara had introduced as being a pupil on
the Donat estate.

After the dance he sat out with her until Luke Donat
approached, when he bowed with old-fashioned courtesy
and moved away.

The coal-black eyes of the other youth appraised Hope
boldly. 'So you are the English cousin of my little partner? Which of your boy-friends brought you along to this
hop?' he demanded.

'Boy-friend? I haven't one. I came with Mrs Paul,'
Hope told him.

'No boy-friend? Too bad. Then I'm not cutting in on one if I suggest we dance. Care to?'

The invitation was too offhand for Hope's liking, but she had no reason for refusing. The band was playing a tango and he guided her through it with superb expertise. When the rhythm changed to an insistent pop beat, he released her and embarked on an advance-and-retreat movement, inviting her to copy it and to invent steps of her own. Moving leisurely towards her and away, he managed to make conversation.

'Where have you been hiding since you came out?' he asked.

Hope told him and he agreed that Tina had said so already. 'You should have got your chief to find you some place in town. You'd have had more fun,' he advised.

'I think I'm going to enjoy being where I am,' said Hope.

'And trust Napier to see that you don't get *too* much fun. According to your cousin, he practically rang a curfew for her every night.'

Hope laughed. 'I'm afraid Tina exaggerates a lot.' To change the subject she asked, 'What do you do yourself?'

'Do?' As if he thought he was answering her question, 'My father owns the Planchet estate,' he said.

'Yes, but you——?'

He shrugged. 'Sail. Swim. Ride. Play around generally. Any of all that on your own programe?'

'Only swimming.'

'Well, that will do for a start. Where do you swim?'

'I haven't been here for a week. I haven't done any yet.' Hope's glance had noticed Tina sitting alone and watching their antics intently, her pretty face sullen. Tina was registering jealousy of her partner and Hope had no wish to detain him. She stood still and he moved with her off the floor.

'What's wrong?' His tone was truculent. 'Don't you fancy my dancing? Or have you got a date with some bigger fish?'

'Of course not. I've enjoyed it. But the band does rather go *on*, doesn't it?' She sat down, while he stood with a foot on the rung of her chair.

'In other words, you are sending me back to duty with young Tina?' he demanded shrewdly.

'Well, she isn't dancing at the moment, and you did come with her.'

'None of my doing, inviting her. She was wished on me by Victoire de Faye, and after all, I'll try anything once. Won't *you*?'

'It depends on what it is.'

'Chicken!' he jeered at her. 'Anyway, it was doing them both a kindness to take Tina off Victoire's hands. Because Victoire, it's been obvious for some time, is breathing rather heavily in Napier's direction, so that relieving her of her little protegée for even one evening was a charity, as I saw it.'

So Tina must have based her speculations on island gossip, thought Hope. But scorning to discuss them with him, she advised instead, 'Well, duty-escort or no, don't you think you owe Tina some more of your company now?'

'Wanting my honest opinion on that?' he quipped.

'Not particularly. Simply telling you that *I* think you do,' she said, frank because, with anyone of his thick skin, she felt she must be.

He looked at her, impervious to the snub. Then, with pseudo-gallantry, he clicked his heels and sketched a

salute. 'Yes, ma'am. Or correct me, do! Should it be
schoolmarm?' he mocked her as he slid lithely away.

Glad to be rid of him, Hope watched his return to Tina
and saw them both go towards the buffet. She sat alone
until she began to feel conspicuous, and was about to seek
the cloakroom when Craig Napier came up to her.

'Will you dance?' he asked.

She was glad when, on the floor, his hand went firmly
to her back, drawing her close. She would have felt self-
conscious, executing with him the impromptu capers she
had shared with Luke Donat, and once she began to
follow Craig's lead, she realised that dancing with him
meant at his explicit guidance and control. He danced as
she suspected he did most things—with the bland assurance that he knew very well what he was about, and at
least in dancing it made partnering him very pleasurable.
It was good to be led where he wanted, turned at his
scarcely perceptible touch, swept and swayed this way
and that, always at his interpretation of what the dance
should be. While it lasted, it made one entity of the two
of them. Or was that, she wondered, to see herself as a
kind of puppet, jerking to his pull on the strings? But she
rejected the thought. Dancing in partnership *ought* to be
like that, and nowadays too often wasn't. She wished this
dance hadn't to come to an end.

Craig said, 'You and Barbara should have come with
our party. But you seem to have made some contacts of
your own. You even filched Tina's escort from her, which
couldn't have pleased her overmuch.'

'Only for one dance,' Hope pointed out.

'No more? She seemed to be sitting alone for rather a
long time, looking as if the law of the jungle was operat-
ing strongly in your favour and against her.'

'Tch! That's nonsense.' Though Hope knew Tina had radiated jealousy, she was not going to admit as much to him. 'Tina couldn't be so petty as to mind my dancing once with Luke Donat. Besides, she's had plenty of other partners tonight, and no one expects to dance *every* time——' Hope checked there, realising too late that that sounded as if she were admitting and excusing herself for usurping Luke Donat; also, from Craig's expression, that he thought the same. But all he said with pseudo-mildness was, 'You don't have to *apologise* for jungle law, you know. It's been universally around for far too long, and you probably wouldn't be feminine if you couldn't argue your right to make use of it now and again.'

Which meant, Hope thought, seething, that he hadn't believed a single word of her denial that she had deliberately kept Luke Donat from Tina. Jungle law, indeed—as if she would ever be in competition for a man with a kitten like Tina! Just how little dignity did he suppose she had?

When the music slowed and stopped a few minutes later, he said, 'I've already collected Barbara and her partner for supper, and you must join us too.'

Hope hung back, foreseeing the inevitable cross-currents of hostility between Victoire de Faye and Barbara at which Tina had hinted. 'Oh——' she began. 'Barbara and I had arranged to meet for supper, I think she meant——'

'Rubbish,' Craig cut in. 'She's with her partner, Edward Rippon, and they've already accepted, so if you don't, what do you propose to do? Chew a crust in a corner, solo? Don't be difficult, please. Come along.'

He led the way to a table near the buffet where Victoire de Faye was about to seat herself. At sight of Hope with

Craig and Barbara she hesitated, then said, 'I have changed my mind, Craig, about staying for this. I should like you to take me home.'

He drew out chairs for Barbara and Hope before he replied. Then, calmly, 'When you've had something to eat. What may I bring you?' he asked.

She frowned. 'I said I wanted to leave now. Didn't you hear me? Or are you suggesting I go alone?'

'You haven't your car. I brought you in mine.'

'And so?'

'And so I hope you'll let me drive you back as soon as you like after supper. Meanwhile, please don't spoil the party.' He stood by her chair until she sat down with obvious ill grace, acknowledging the others with a nod shared between them.

She toyed with smoked salmon and sipped a little wine while for the most part, the men talked between themselves and to Barbara and Hope. She addressed Barbara once on some triviality and condescended to Hope, 'Barbara should have found a partner for you. So humiliating, I always feel, for a girl to have to depend on the odd, casual invitation to dance,' making Hope aware that she had been noticed and pitied while she had sat alone after Luke Donat had left her.

Altogether the supper session was an uneasy one, and Hope was not sorry when Barbara suggested they leave after it. While Barbara said goodnight to her partner Hope heard Craig ask Victoire, 'If I'm to take you home now, what about Tina?'

Victoire shrugged. 'What about her? She came with Luke Donat. She can go back with him.'

'Not,' returned Craig firmly, 'after you've already left.'

'Why not? She is not a child.'

'All the same, you should know as well as I do that going out for the evening and coming home from it are two different things to Donat. If you're determined to go now, he and Tina are not to outstay you,' he retorted.

Another shrug. 'If they want to, how can I stop them?'

'*I* can. They'll come,' said Craig, conviction in his tone. As he turned away, adding, 'When you're ready, I'll join you at the car after I've seen them into Donat's,' Hope realised she had glimpsed a facet of his character which she liked. He had little use for Tina, as she knew, but he showed almost a guardian's concern for her as a girl. More, certainly, than did her new hostess, Victoire. It was obvious too that he didn't trust Luke Donat. And in that, on the little evidence she had, Hope agreed with him.

On their own way home Barbara said, 'Victoire makes things very difficult for Craig.'

'You mean her wanting to leave when, as she was already at the table, he must have been expecting her to stay? I'm afraid she reminded me of a child saying, "I was going to play; now I shan't," just to be awkward,' Hope remarked.

'Yes—when she found he'd invited us to eat with them; when she had thought they were to be tête-à-tête and realised that they weren't. More than that, she had to be reasonably polite to me in front of Edward Rippon and you. In front of Craig, she doesn't always bother to try.'

Hope was silent, piecing this into Tina's pronouncement that Victoire and Barbara did not 'get on'. Dared she ask Barbara why? Instead she compressed with, 'Doesn't Madame de Faye like you, then?'

'Doesn't she make it rather obvious?' There was an unwontedly bitter note in Barbara's voice.

'She did tonight,' Hope admitted. 'But do you know why?'

'Yes.' Almost echoing Tina, Barbara added, 'She hates me—with reason, she thinks,' speaking now with a finality which Hope felt she must not question. Whatever the cause of the other woman's enmity, it was clear that Barbara knew it for an injustice, the wound of which went deep.

CHAPTER FOUR

TINA lost no time in making a double errand of showing off her new toy to Hope and of airing a grievance on the subject of Luke Donat. She drove over to the bungalow on the Sunday.

Hope admired the car and asked when Tina's small charge was expected to arrive.

'Crispin? Early next week,' Tina said, and then, 'Luke Donat said you made a big thing of pitying me for not getting a partner while he was dancing with you; that, though you told him you wanted him to stay with you, you went all heroic and sent him back to me. Did you?'

'I don't know what he meant by "a big thing", nor why he lied that I wanted to keep him,' returned Hope. 'He's a very good dancer, I'll give you that, but I didn't find him attractive. You could have had him back, as far as I was concerned, at any time you wanted.'

'But you did send him?' Tina pressed. 'You *humiliated* me by sending him?'

'Oh, don't be so touchy,' Hope urged. 'He came back to you, didn't he—lies and all? But look, are you going to give me a run in the car or not?'

It seemed that Tina's pride of possession was too much for her ill-humour. 'All right,' she grudged. 'Where do you want to go? Shall we swim? If so, where?'

'At Cloud's Nest?' Hope suggested. 'It's beautifully quiet there.'

On the way she told Tina of Barbara's advice to keep a

swim-suit at the office and to slip over to the coast some-times in the long lunch break.

Tina pursed her lips. 'If you can get away with it.'

'If——? What do you mean?'

'That you'll be lucky if the Ogre doesn't find a very special job for you to do on the day you plan to go, and whether or not you get a break, he couldn't care less. *Or* if you're late back, as I was once, when I came into town with a couple of girls from the *boucan,* then the angels had better be on your side, that's all.'

Hope leaned forward to flick a finger on the dash-board. 'Touch wood, I needn't ever be late back. Any time I thought there was any risk, I needn't go. But norm-ally there should be bags of time.'

As it happened, she chose the following Thursday, a day of rich heat, when the sea seemed to beckon. As she wheeled out her scooter and prepared to mount, Craig was going to his car.

'Where are you bound?' he asked.

'To Cloud's Nest bay for a swim.'

'Alone?'

'I've got a book and a picnic lunch.'

He nodded and she rode away, revelling in the sun, the warm wind in her face, and, at the back of her mind, in the quiet confidence that already she was getting on top of the job, loving its novelty and its challenge to her skills. How many days had she been working for Craig Napier? Only five? And already she knew she was going to hate having to hand over to anyone else when the time came—as she supposed it must.

She was remembering her small shock at Barbara's question as to whether she was going to like Craig. Not ready to answer it, she had turned her reply, and even now 'like' didn't seem quite the right word.

Respect? Admire? No, they weren't right either. Revere, then? Heavens, that was much too worshipful! So from like, where did one go next? Fleetingly her thought suggested love, and at that she threw back her head and laughed aloud. That *would* be the cardinal error—to flatter the man's ego as those other misguided females had done! Certainly he had agreed that she wasn't likely to commit it. But she could still recall his caustic exit-line of that first night—'Remember, won't you, that you've been warned?'

She found the wide crescent of the bay deserted, but for a group of Creole boys playing at the edge of the surf, far down the beach, from where their raised voices barely reached her. She parked her scooter in the shade of some trees on the dunes above the beach, slipped out of the dress under which she wore her one-piece suit, kicked off her sandals and ran down to the water's edge.

She swam, floated, did some porpoise dives and rode the occasional long roller which came in. Then, hungry for her lunch, she collected it from her scooter and settled to eat it under a big tree, wind-slanted towards the sea, which bore a scatter of fruits of the greenish-gold of a pippin. Afterwards, because she was in danger of drowsing into sleep, she swam again, calculating that when she came out, there would be to spare about the half-hour she would need for getting back to the office.

She walked up the beach, so dazzled by the sun that she did not notice someone was sitting near her towel and sandals. Closer she recognised Luke Donat, whose arrival she was not at all disposed to welcome.

'Hi!' he greeted her, without rising.

'Hallo,' she said, picking up her towel and beginning to dry her legs.

'Surprised to see me?'

'Yes.'

'You haven't felt you should make up to me for the way you dismissed me the other night? And you give me no credit for troubling to find out where I could see you again, and when?'

'Credit? I certainly don't know why you bothered, but I think I can bear not to know,' she said indifferently.

'Though I daresay you can guess. Tina told me, of course, and believe it or not, I've been down here every day this week without success until now.'

'Really?' In putting on one sandal she nearly overbalanced, and was able to make little resistance when he pulled her down beside him.

'Sit for that,' he advised. 'It's easier than playing heron.'

With both sandals on, she said, 'I must go now,' and made to get up. But he pinioned her wrist while his bold eyes looked her figure over.

'You can't go yet. You're still wet,' he said.

'By the time I've collected my things, I shall be dry enough to put on my dress over my suit.'

'Things? What things? Where did you leave them?'

'My book and my lunch-box. I ate my lunch under that tree——' She pointed back to it, and he turned.

'*That* one? The manchineel? Well, I hope you didn't play Eve and help yourself to one of the fruits for dessert? But obviously not, or you wouldn't have been mermaiding since.'

Intrigued against her will, she knelt up, looking at the tree. 'Why shouldn't I?' she asked.

'Rank poison. Leaves, bark, fruit—the lot. One bite,

and your throat swells up; one touch of the leaves and
your hands are a mass of blisters. When they cut one of
them down, they have to burn the juice from the bark
first, or it can blind.'

'And it's a—what? A manchineel? But why are they
allowed to grow at all? Why aren't they all cut down?'

'The wood is too valuable; it takes a high polish. And
now, in return for that piece of nature lore, you are going
to stay for a while, aren't you?'

'No, I can't. I must go, or I shall be late.'

He followed her up the beach and over the sand-
hummocks to where she had left the scooter. His car
stood out on the road, but the scooter wasn't there.

She turned to him. 'It's gone! It's been stolen!' she
gasped.

She was puzzled by his smile. 'Not stolen,' he said. 'Just
—lent. For a joy-ride. You'll get it back. In fact, it just
could be back at your Belle Rose office by now. Or not—
depending how long the joy-ride may have taken.'

'Wh-what do you mean?' Hope was stammering with
rage. '*You* lent it to someone? To prevent my getting
back on it myself?'

Luke nodded. 'To one of them,' he gestured down the
beach towards the group of boys. 'They're field lads from
Planchet, having a day off. Money passed, and I gave him
an hour in which to have a ride around and deliver the
thing back in good order. Back on Belle Rose; *not* back
here. Fair enough, I argued, to give us time to play a
bit—because I'm prepared to swim too—and afterwards
I'd take you back by car, and no harm done.'

'No *harm*? Don't you realise that I'm almost late already? And if you think I'd accept a lift from you after
this——!' she stormed.

'And what alternative have you, milady?'

'I'll walk.'

'Go ahead. It's all of twelve kilometres.'

'I'll hitch a lift.'

'You'll be lucky—in mid-afternoon, when all good Madeninans sleep. Now be sensible. Get into the car, and I'll drive you back—*when* I'm so disposed.'

She gritted her teeth. 'You'll go now!'

'And who's going to make me?' Luke dangled his car-keys at her. 'We'll go when I say so, not before.'

She got in and he took the driver's seat. They sat in stony silence while the precious minutes ticked by. At last he said, 'So—forfeit paid for the moment. Let's go.'

On the way Hope debated what chance she had of getting to her desk without Craig's learning how late she was. But almost at once she despised such a ruse. She *wanted* to justify herself to him; she *wanted* him to hear of Luke's low trick. So when they arrived she was not too sorry to see his car outside the office and her scooter near by. For that meant he must have learned part of the story, if not all.

As soon as the car stopped she was out of it. Luke Donat called after her, 'I'll stick around. Call me if you need help, won't you?' Whereat she turned on him.

'You'll not stick around. You'll scram, do you hear?' she ordered. 'And don't try anything of the sort again with me—ever!'

He laughed unpleasantly. 'Why, you don't think I was really after the company of a prude like you?' he jeered. 'You must think we've a famine in girls around here, and we haven't. But once a snooty like you tries to come the heavy aunt and dictate my duty to me, she's likely to get the same treatment—or worse. So good luck to you with your boss. You'll probably need it. He has the reputation of eating secretaries for breakfast and there's no reason that I can see why he shouldn't fry *you*!'

Furious to the point of having no retort ready, Hope left him to drive away. When she went through to the office Craig was moving to his desk from the window, and she realised he must have witnessed the scene outside.

She put a hand to her flushed cheek, then brushed back her wild hair. 'I'm terribly sorry, but it wasn't my——' She stopped, daunted by the expression on Craig's face. Seated at his desk now, he looked up at her, *through* her.

'You realise, I hope, that it's Thursday, and you haven't done the pay-slips yet?' he said.

'Yes, of course. I'll do them and finish them before I go.'

'You certainly will.'

'Yes, but—Look, you must let me explain first why I'm late——'

His brows drew together. ' "Must"—when I know most of it already? That you had a date to keep, and kept it, after lying to me that you would be spending the time alone. That when you'd taken more time than you were entitled to, you or Donat sent your machine back by the lad, knowing that Donat could get you back quicker in his car, *when* you were able to tear yourself away. Well, anything you want to add to that? Or subtract from it, if I haven't got all the details right?'

Hope had to swallow hard on the constriction in her throat. Of all wrongs she could bear injustice the least, and that he should dare to prejudge her was too much!

'Details?' she echoed thickly. 'You haven't got *any* of it right. It wasn't like that at all!'

'Oh, come!' he urged.

'No! For one thing, I didn't lie to you. I was going
alone, and I didn't expect—that is, I hadn't any rendezvous planned with Luke Donat. He——'

'Just turned up by mere chance? But knowing where to
find you, no doubt?'

'Yes, but——'

'Then need we belabour the thing any more? He persuaded you to overstay your time, and you stayed. What's
more, you didn't noticeably hurry your leavetakings when
you did part from the fellow. Meanwhile, I'm not interested in the embroidery of the affair, and I'd be grateful now if you'd get down to your job.'

But that she could not do in dumb obedience to his
say-so. How dared he dismiss her explanations almost as
if she hadn't spoken? Well, she *would* speak now, and he
was *going* to listen, if not to any further attempts to
justify herself, at least to some home-truths which it was
high time he heard!

Gathering her forces, she said, 'No. If you still wish it,
I'll get down to my job when I've said this, and not before. This being that I consider your attitude unjust and
autocratic and totally unfair in the circumstances. And
though I've no intention of urging any more "embroidery" upon you, I think you should know just how
well I'm beginning to understand my cousin's estimate of
you as a—a tyrant whom she could never manage to
please. And furthermore——' she hesitated, despising an
increasing quiver in her voice, but plunging on regard-
less—'furthermore, if you treated any of your earlier
secretaries like this, I simply can't credit that they could
have imagined themselves in love with you, as you claim.
They must have been out of their minds, or *you* must
have been mistaken!'

She had gone too far, and she knew it. These were gutter tactics, but the words were out; she couldn't recall them, and her heart was thumping furiously as she forced her eyes to meet the cold pebble-green of his. The blackness behind the green flecks was unfathomable.

'Have you finished?' he asked.

On an already dying defiance, 'Isn't that enough?' she retorted.

'Entirely. A great deal too much, as I think you must know. And all of it a pettiness which I'm not going to answer. And so——'

With what seemed like a single stride he was on her side of his desk again, and his hand, vice-like in its grip, was on her shoulder, thrusting her towards her own desk and holding her down in her chair when she half-attempted to rise. 'And so now you *will* get on with your work until you have finished it. And no—hot and dishevelled you may be from heaven knows what erotic acrobatics you and your boy-friend may have been indulging in, but you will refrain from going to the cloakroom to repair the ravages until *after* you've finished here. Then, and only then, we'll consider the incident of your lateness closed. Understood?' he demanded savagely.

She had to obey. Back at his desk now, working at his papers, he did not once glance her way. He might have been alone in the room, and when he went out once, he did not, as usual, tell her where he could be found if he were wanted.

She felt ostracised—for the comparatively simple fault of being late on duty. She had been taking his dictation most of the morning; he knew she had the pay-slips to do, and he must knew he could trust her to finish them before she went home. He didn't have to make a threat of it! As she worked, her sense of frustration and grievance rose. And yet, oddly, she felt less aggrieved with Craig than with herself. *She* should have seen that he couldn't possibly think her as irresponsible as Tina; *she* should have convinced him that she wouldn't stoop to hiding behind a lie. Didn't she convey *any* candour in her face, in her voice? And though her reason argued, 'You've only been working for the man a week. How can you expect him to know you for what you really are?' she was still aware of the nag of this illogical self-blame for having failed to show him what she was. For having failed him ...

Before she had finished the pay-slips she heard the other clerks leave the building and flutter away. She was punching the completed pile when Craig returned and, remembering her last Thursday's errand, she asked, 'Shall I take them down to the *boucan* now?'

'No. The bank will have closed by the time Winston will have checked them. He can have them in the morning. That's all, then. Goodnight.'

It was a dismissal of her which daunted any further attempt to put herself right with him, so she merely returned his goodnight and left him.

On the ride home she contrasted her low spirits with her sunny mood of the morning, her one consolation being that at least she could hope for Barbara's sympathetic ear for the truth of her story. It was not until she was putting her scooter away that she knew she wasn't going to mention the incident to Barbara. For Barbara might want to plead her case with Craig, and Hope's pride wasn't having that. She would fight her own battles with him without even Barbara's help.

Even if she had not so decided, she would have been daunted by Barbara's mood that evening. Usually she greeted Hope sunnily and had a long, cold drink ready for her. But tonight she called from her room to ask Hope to pour her own, and at supper she was obviously tense and so withdrawn that Hope asked if she were not well.

Barbara said, 'It's nothing. Just a slight headache, that's all, and I'm not used to them.' But instead of joining Hope on the verandah when they had cleared the meal, she went to the telephone and came back to suggest diffidently that as Craig was coming over and they had some private business, perhaps when he came, Hope wouldn't mind leaving them alone.

Hope agreed readily to go to her room and hastened to absent herself before Craig arrived. But after she knew he had come, she felt tempted by the velvet dusk to go for a walk. She could leave by a side door and could get back to her room by the same way if he were still there when she returned.

She walked down the road in the opposite direction from which his car had come. On either side sandy paths led away into low-growing scrub and, following one of them, she was grateful for the solitude of the Madenina countryside at night. She had learned from Barbara that, except on party or carnival evenings, most of the islanders kept the early hours which their ancestors had done—at both ends of the day. In the country, very few people were abroad much later than an hour after the sun had gone down, so that for anyone walking alone there was no need to listen for the sinister following footsteps or see a threat in a shadow behind a tree. And the silence was broken by little other than the chirrup of the tree-frogs and the rustle of the wind in bamboo and the high palms.

On Madenina the dark never came down as suddenly as Hope's reading and hearsay had led her to expect. To her, the sinking ball of the sun seemed to take a great while over its going, and for a long time afterwards left the sky streaked with crimson and gold which only slowly turned to grey and then to night.

She remembered asking Barbara about the elusive green ray which was supposed to appear at the very last instant of the tropical sun's sinking. 'Have you ever seen it?' she had queried.

'Of course,' Barbara had said, adding with what sounded to Hope like inconsequence, 'I am a Madeninan.'

'What has that to do with the green ray?' Hope had puzzled.

'Oh——' Barbara had laughed. 'Well, it's said that you can't count yourself as a true Madeninan until you *have* seen it, though, believe it or not, I know people who never have. Victoire de Faye, for one. But then she makes rather a pride of not being one of us.'

Hope had said, 'Tina tells me she's never seen it. And I don't suppose I shall either.'

'Why not?'

'Well, how much of a rarity is it? Shouldn't I be lucky to see it, just in the time I shall be here?'

'You never know,' Barbara had advised. 'It might show up for you this very evening. And if not, as long as you look out for it, you'll be very *un*lucky if you don't see it sooner or later.'

Hope stayed out for the best part of an hour. When she drew near to the bungalow she saw Craig's car still outside it, and silhouetted in the open doorway were his figure and Barbara's, as if he were on the point of leaving.

That gave Hope no chance or reaching the side door unseen, so she stepped back into the shadow of a crape myrtle tree, watching until Craig should leave. But as she watched she saw Barbara's hands go to his shoulders, and as she hid her face on his breast his arms went about her, drawing her close.

Hope drew a sharp breath, her guilt that of an eavesdropper, and some feeling which she did not understand quickening her heartbeat as if in shock.

Why was that? She had known since first meeting them together that Barbara and Craig were close. Barbara's warmth in speaking of him had confirmed it and so had Tina's oblique hints. Tonight, when Barbara had obviously been distressed, she had turned to him, and if they were indeed lovers, what more natural than such a parting between them?

Yet Hope's recoil from it dismayed her. She pitied Barbara's young widowhood, admired her courage, liked her, wanted her to be happy again—surely?

But happy with Craig Napier? In spite of her question to Tina—why not?—did she unreservedly want that for Barbara? Or was her reluctance to face facts the stirring of something else? Something that was not jealousy, but *was* an envy of the rapport the other girl had with him, an envy which was almost a hunger to know she could count on as much of his understanding as Barbara could.

That meant—But no, how could it mean that in this short time of knowing the man she wanted from him the love and tenderness he showed to Barbara? At the thought, though her reason rejected its absurdity, her honesty admitted that she could not have been so hurt by his misjudgment of her that afternoon if nothing in her feminine make-up had responded to the challenge of his maleness. If the makings of the spark were not there, she could have witnessed this scene tonight with complete *sangfroid*; she could have felt wholeheartedly glad for

Barbara, and she had not. The spark was there, but it must be quenched. For, lit and allowed to glow in fantasy, it spelled danger. She heard again his caustic, 'You have been warned', and the echo was like the spray of a cold shower upon her wistful thinking. She *had* to be glad for Barbara. She herself wasn't even in the same scene.

After Craig had driven away she waited for some time, lest Barbara should conclude she had been near enough to see her with Craig at the door. Or, better still, if Barbara had already gone to her room, she might get to her own without their meeting. But they met in the narrow hall between their rooms and even by the soft light of the lamp there, Hope could see that Barbara had been crying.

'Business' with Craig? No. Trouble, then? But Barbara's stricken look daunted Hope's asking if there was anything she could do to help. So she merely said she had been out for a walk and answered No, that she had loved it, to Barbara's lack-lustre query as to whether she hadn't been afraid, alone in the dark.

That was all. They said their goodnights and went to their rooms.

The next day Hope found that her vague misgivings and self-questions were not proof against the clear beauty of a Madeninian morning, and Barbara's mood seemed brighter too. And evidently Craig possessed a detachment which could cut off each day's frictions from those of the next, for his manner with Hope was as coolly positive as ever. Nothing of yesterday's clash might ever have happened, and in face of his demands on her time, she almost succeeded in putting her last night's awareness of his magnetism behind her. If he wanted a robot for a secretary, then a robot she must try to be!

And it was to seem that not only to Craig was she invisible as a woman, when Victoire de Faye came into the office, according her a mere nod before addressing Craig.

'I must ask you to meet Crispin at the airport when he arrives,' she told Craig. 'I'm flying down to Barbados for three days, to do some shopping and to get my hair done, and I shan't be back until that evening.'

Craig remarked, 'I thought that was to be Tina Godwin's function—to cope with Crispin for you?'

'She can begin when we get back. I am taking her with me to run errands for me while I am down there.'

'Then the idea is that I deliver Crispin to the House, without either of you being there?'

Victoire frowned. 'Don't make a grievance of my being away, *please*. Sinbad and Doria will be there to give him a meal, and I shall be back on the evening plane.'

'Very well. I'll lay it on,' Craig promised. He looked across at Hope. 'Make a note in the diary, will you? What time is he supposed to arrive? I suppose he'll be in the charge of the stewardess, won't he?' he asked Victoire.

More than once during the next few days Hope made a point of going over to the coast in the lunch-break and seeing to it that she was punctually at her desk again by three o'clock. Once, she heard from one of the other girls, Craig had been enquiring for her at half-past two, and had been told where the girl thought she had gone. But on her return he made no remark, except to say he had some urgent letters to dictate, and had hoped to find her in the canteen.

During those same days, as far as she knew, he did not visit the bungalow, nor did Barbara mention him to Hope, whose puzzled thoughts could not make their loving parting and Barbara's tears into any pattern which

seemed to fit their relationship. Last weekend, for instance
—Hope's first on the island—Craig had lunched and
stayed for supper with Barbara. Yet this Sunday she suggested she and Hope should take a picnic in the moun-
tains, and they only did not go because it rained for most
of the daylight hours.

On the day Crispin de Faye was to fly in Craig demanded Hope's help with him. (Why hadn't Craig asked
Barbara?) 'On his first day, the kid deserves better than
to be left in charge of a couple of servants to rattle around
the house until Victoire comes home,' Craig claimed, and
drove Hope with him to the airport when the child's
plane was due.

For a boy who was nearing nine, Crispin looked young
for his age. He was small, with an olive skin and delicate
features under a thatch of dark hair. He spoke English
with very little accent, which surprised Hope, as she had
assumed until then that, while Victoire had been in Paris,
he had attended a French school.

'No,' Craig told her as he introducd him to her. 'He's
been at the English-French Lycée in London. Roland
wanted that for him—that he should be bi-lingual, which
Roland himself never quite managed to be.'

Crispin shook hands with Hope. 'You're not the same
secretary as Uncle Craig had when we went away,' he ob-
servèd.

Craig slanted a glance at Hope. 'Not the same by
several samples, tell him,' he advised.

Crispin was looking about him. 'Where is Belle-mère?'
he asked.

'She had to go to Barbados, but she'll be home tonight.
Meanwhile I'm lending Hope to you, so see that you keep
her amused, will you?'

'Thank you. But I daresay I could have managed with Sadie and Matthew-John until Belle-mère comes back.'

'Yes, well'—They were in the car-park now, and Craig was stowing Crispin's holdalls—'the fact is, fellow, that Sadie and her husband aren't at the House any more,' he said.

Crispin's eyes widened and the corners of his mouth came down. 'Not *there* any more?' he echoed. 'But they were! They always have been—What do you mean—not there?'

'They had to leave after your stepmother closed the house down. They took places as cook and man over at Montgaye. They would like to see you if you went over there, I'm pretty sure. You must ask Tina to take you.'

'Who is Tina?' asked Crispin.

Driving away, Craig left Hope to explain Tina to him. As they neared the estate he began to notice and point out landmarks, and he waved to the groups of West Indian boys they passed on the road. He asked after some of the estate's dogs he had known, and when they reached his home he claimed wistfully, 'If Sadie and Matthew-John knew I was coming, they would have been out on the terrace to meet me.'

But there was no one to greet him, either there or in the big hall, which struck coldly after the warmth out of doors. The rest of the house seemed strangely silent too, the explanation of which Craig brought back with him after he had gone through to the kitchen quarters.

'Victoire's couple have skipped it for the day,' he told Hope. 'They left a note for her. Read it.'

Hope read, 'Missus, gone up-island see our cousin. Back 'long time you home.' It was signed 'Doria' in clumsy capitals.

'What does "'long time" mean? "Before"?' Hope asked

'More "about the same time",' Craig said. 'That means the evening, and it looks as if either Victoire hadn't told them to expect Crispin this morning, or as if they couldn't have cared less.' He turned to Crispin. 'When did you last eat?'

'There was breakfast on the plane.'

'So what were you fancying for lunch?'

'Curry,' said Crispin promptly.

Craig lifted an eyebrow in Hope's direction. 'Curry? Uncharted country to you? Or could you produce one?'

'Given some ingredients, I think I could,' she said. 'Onions, butter, some cooked meats, stock, rice, curry powder, mango chutney——'

He grimaced. 'Heavens, what a list! But let's see what the kitchen can offer.'

There were no suitable cooked meats, but there was a large container of fresh prawns. Remembering that in Madenina they were shrimps, 'Would you settle for curried shrimps?' she asked Crispin.

'Curried anything,' he assented cheerfully. At which Craig suggested taking him out on to the estate, leaving Hope to work alone. She told them she would need at least an hour, for curry must cook slowly.

There was no chutney, but she mashed a couple of ripe mangoes to pulp and added a little vinegar and lemon juice. There was rice and a spicy curry powder, and a very passable curry had evolved by the time the other two returned, Craig bringing a bottle of wine from his own quarters, and there was lime-juice for Crispin.

Not caring to use Victoire's table appointments, Hope served it in the servants' front kitchen, thinking as she laid the cutlery and glass that the last thing she had expected of today was to be serving to her chief an improvised meal which she had cooked herself.

Craig queried, '*Haute cusine* among your other efficiencies?' To which, a little headily, she replied, 'You consider I have some others?' and took his casual, 'I've remarked one or two, here and there,' as praise of talents which he seemed to think he had the right to expect and to take completely for granted.

Afterwards he left, saying he would come back in the evening to drive Hope home. The other two found that Crispin's room and playroom had been made ready for him, which showed that only the servants had been irresponsible about his arrival. Victoire must have given them their orders.

When Hope asked Crispin what he would like to do, he replied, 'Draw,' with as single-minded conviction as he had demanded curry.

'What with?' Hope asked. 'Have you pencils and paper?'

'In my valise. I'll unpack them.'

'I nearly always draw boats,' he announced, and as Hope sat and watched, certainly some recognisable craft appeared on the paper.

There were dinghies and yachts, an ocean-going ship and a catamaran. On the deck of one of the yachts he had pencilled in some matchstick human figures—three of them.

'That's Papa and Uncle Nelson and Uncle Craig,' he pointed out. 'They used to sail together, and sometimes I went too. But on board I had to wear a rope tied to my belt, like a dog on a lead.' He sat back, surveying his work, then took up his eraser and bent again over the sketch. Using the rubber on one of the figures, he said, 'That's wrong for the day when the hurricane wrecked the boat and Papa and Uncle Nelson didn't come back. Uncle Craig wasn't there, so I shouldn't have drawn him in the picture, should I?'

Hope said, 'Not if you meant to draw that day. But wouldn't you rather draw a happier one—when Mr Napier might have been there?'

Still scrubbing at the paper, Crispin agreed, 'I do, sometimes. But *this* picture is that day—look at all the storm-clouds coming up. And that day Uncle Craig wasn't there. He had stayed behind. He was at Uncle Nelson's apartment in town—with Aunty Barbara.' He paused. Then, 'Belle-mère was *very* angry,' he added, telling Hope in all innocence things she did not care to know.

CHAPTER FIVE

CRAIG had not said he meant to collect Victoire and Tina at the airport, but when he came back in the evening for Hope he brought them with him in his car. Meanwhile the truant servants had not yet returned, and Hope did not envy them Victoire's reception of them when they did show up.

Craig did nothing for her fury by suggesting she would have done better by keeping on or taking back Sadie and Matthew-John Bosun, who had been loyal to the Great House for years.

She turned on him. 'How could I keep them on? I was closing the house!'

'They'd have been glad to take board-wages until you came back.'

'You know I hadn't decided whether I *was* coming back,' Victoire snapped.

'But when you did, they would have come back to you, if you'd made it worth their while.'

'By doubling their pay, I suppose? Allowing them to blackmail me. No, thank you. When I have to creep to my domestic staff——! Anyway, as I have no intention of getting my own dinner, you can take me out. I can leave Crispin with Tina; she will put him to bed.'

Craig said, 'I have to take Hope home.'

'—To the Poisson d'or, I think. It's the "in" place this season. I'll have changed and be nearly ready by the time you come back. If I'm not, you will have to wait until I am.'

For a long moment Craig did not reply. Then he said quietly, 'Sometimes, Victoire, you ride your privileges as if they were rights, don't you?'

Her eyes narrowed. 'And what do you mean by that?'

He did not tell her. 'I'll pick you up in half an hour,' he said, and ushered Hope from the room.

When he asked her how she and Crispin had occupied themselves during the afternoon, she told him that after the drawing-session they had played Draughts and Snap, at both of which she had been heavily outclassed. Too dismayed by the child's artless candour, she reported nothing about the subject of his drawing, and would not have mentioned it to Barbara either if, that night, Barbara had not asked, seeming to know what her answer would be.

Barbara nodded. 'Since his father was lost, he has always wanted to draw boats with people aboard. At first, I think, it was because he wouldn't accept that Roland and Nelson weren't still afloat somewhere and would come back. And now that he's had to believe it, as we all have, it could be his way of working the tragedy out of his system. At least, that's what I've hoped if he wants to draw boats whenever he is with me.'

'You could be right. He spoke to me quite calmly about his father. Does he often come over to see you?' Hope asked.

'Before he went away to school, Craig would sometimes bring him, whether or not with Victoire's permission, I never made myself ask,' Barbara admitted. 'I shan't either, if Craig brings him this time,' she added, causing Hope to wonder whether Barbara was reluctant to acknowledge how many fewer were Craig's brief calls lately, even on legitimate errands, such as his driving back with Hope herself tonight.

Christmas came quietly to the island, with little of the frenzied commercials and ritual feasting which led up to and away from it in England. There were parties in the tourist hotels and the cruise-ships which put in at Fort Belain and stayed over for two or three days. By contrast, the French Caribbean islands made more of the Jour de l'An, New Year's Day, when Madenina went *en fête,* with all the shops closed, all the bars open, no work being done on the sugar-plantations nor in the cocoa-groves, and consequently many a hangover to follow.

'It acts as a kind of trial run for the Mardi Gras Carnival which explodes just before Lent. On Fat Tuesday and Ash Wednesday, particularly on Wednesday, when they celebrate the death of Vaval, the island's private devil, you'll really see something of Madenina gone mad,' Craig told Hope, assuming, she realised, that she would still be there so far ahead, when by the London office's unwritten agreement with him, she would be back in England, leaving him with a new secretary, trained to his needs.

But when she dutifully broached the subject, he was obstructive.

'I told you when you arrived that I should expect you to stay for as long as I wanted you,' he pointed out.

'And if you remember, I said I couldn't promise to stay indefinitely, if my uncle wanted me back,' Hope said.

'So has he put a limit to your stay?'

In fact, in his last letter and to Hope's relief, Uncle Lionel had pronounced himself well satisfied with Kathy Tremayne's ministrations. So at present she had no reason for making difficulties about staying on; there was only that odd quirk of self-protection which saw the agreement as a way of escape, before working for Craig became too important to her, too dangerously attractive. Therefore, obeying the quirk, she said,

'Not yet. But the idea was, wasn't it, that I was supposed to be training someone else to take my place? And as you hadn't mentioned anything about it, I thought I'd better.'

'Well, forget it, will you?' His tone was dismissive. 'While you suit me, why should I nurse along another tenderfoot, even with your help? So you'll stay, I hope, at least until after the spring *ratoon,* which we can schedule early this year—soon after Mardi Gras is out of the way. So with all due respect, that's what I'd like you to tell your uncle, if he should get restive about you.'

At which the quirk insisted on her asking, 'And after the *ratoon*?'

'We'll play that by ear when the time comes,' he said carelessly and characteristically, settling the point at issue to his convenience; making no enquiry as to how she, personally, was suited with him; treating her as the robot she had resolved to be.

For that *was* Craig; his assurance one of the qualities which a robot could admire, even if a mere woman might crave something less granite-like. Craved it without expecting it. 'Plain janes with their heads screwed on' were supposed to keep their heads that way—especially this one who had been warned, hadn't she, against dreaming romantic dreams?

All the same, just for once she would like to glimpse the softer side of him which Barbara knew and valued—

or had known, before the rift between them, whatever had caused it.

Hope wished she dared ask Barbara about that. But on the subject of Craig there was lately a barrier between the other girl and herself—a barrier that was no more of Barbara's raising than it was of her own reluctance to hear in so many words all that he was or had been to Barbara. Envy of something a friend had and you hadn't gnawed worse, Hope was finding, than outright jealousy of an enemy. It asked more generosity of you; it tore you two ways.

That New Year's Day was a Saturday, and Friday's pay for the week included a special Jour de l'An bonus for each worker. Hope completed and delivered the payslips as usual on Thursday, and having Craig's permission to leave as soon as she had cleared any outstanding correspondence, was on her way to collect her scooter late on Friday afternoon, when a clamour from the direction of the *boucan* assailed her ears, and a shifting, scuffling crowd appeared to be intent on rushing its doors.

Within closer earshot of the noise she halted, staring. The crowd was composed entirely of women and toddler children, their gaudy dresses and head-kerchiefs making a veritable kaleidoscope of colour on the move. At the door of the *boucan* stood Winston Fortune, gesticulating and arguing as he did his best to quell the amazon horde.

Hope moved nearer, near enough to ask what was the matter of a woman who was bobbing and peering over the shoulders of her taller neighbours.

She turned. 'Matter?' she echoed. 'Man Fortune, he won't pay us bonus wages, that matter enough,' she said.

Hope looked at the crowd, remembering the proportion of women workers for whom she made out wage-slips from the payroll, and wondered how it had swelled so suddenly without her knowledge. 'Mr Fortune won't pay you your money?' she questioned. 'Why not?'

A shrug. 'He say, not our money. Wait for men. He say, same every feast-day, and we say he know why. 'Cos men get hands on bonus first, don't give wives their share. We get pay-packet first, we *take* it. But Man Fortune, he won't hand out, not without men here. Not fair.'

Hope began to see light and she sympathised, but obviously she couldn't take sides. If Winston Fortune had the same experience every feast-day eve, she supposed he knew how to cope with it. But curious to learn the rights of the affair, she began to thrust her way through the crowd towards him.

It was not a wise move. For all her gentle 'Excuse-me' touches on arms or backs, it seemed that the mood of the crowd resented her intrusion. She was shouldered and buffeted and the ranks closed in on her, and not only upon her but upon the innocent small targets of the shuffling feet—the children who tagged on to individual skirts amid a forest of them, in danger of being crushed underfoot.

She pushed to more purpose. 'Look out!' she yelled to a near-giantess, whose own foulard head-scarf had been knocked awry. 'You nearly trod on that babe,' Hope accused, and at that moment found herself on her knees, one arm round the tiny's legs, her other hand in sharp agony beneath a heavy sabot-like shoe.

She managed to scramble to her feet, shaking her aching fingers and feeling suddenly sick. Someone took over the child, presumably the mother, for she heard it being comforted in Creole—'*Pov Mamay*'—and the giantess being roundly blamed in the same language. Then Winston

Fortune pushed his way down into the crowd, just as Hope felt a firm hand at her back and Craig was there, cool and authoritative without his having uttered a word.

The clamour died to a murmur and the crowd spread itself more comfortably. Looking about him, Craig chided in a more bantering tone than Hope had ever heard him use, 'Ladies, ladies! Why do we have this *bef duva* effort every feast-day, when you know you can't win?'

This was greeted by a self-conscious chuckle or two and by one reply. 'Bonus belong us. Not man's,' someone said.

'Man has worked to earn bonus as well as pay,' Craig pointed out in the same simple idiom. 'Give you your share every week; don't tell me you not clever enough to coax bonus too!'

At this the chuckles became open guffaws, but the lone complainer came back with, 'Come Jour de l'An, Mardi Gras, Toussaints, he keep bonus, buy rum.'

'And you, madame, never take a little rum yourself, hm?' riposted Craig in a flash, and amid the now totally good-humoured laughter, turned to Winston Fortune at his side.

'The usual—in the canteen,' he said to him, and to the women, 'Coffee for all, ladies—you know where, and Mr Fortune will attend to you, as usual.'

Whatever this cryptic promise conveyed, the crowd broke up at once and streamed away in the direction of the canteen. With a huge shrug Winston Fortune returned to the *boucan*, leaving Craig and Hope standing alone.

He put out his own hand for the one she was nursing. 'Let me see,' he said. She felt her wrist tremble with ner-vous shock as she showed him the torn, bleeding knuckles of her right hand, two of its nails already turning black.

His touch was very gentle. 'Nasty,' he said. 'We must deal with that soonest.'

'When I get home, I'll bathe it in disinfectant and ask Barbara to bandage my fingers,' she promised.

He looked up into her face, 'You'll do nothing of the kind if it involves your riding your machine. You're shocked, and a stiff tot of brandy will take care of that. Come and get into the car. I'll take you back to my place and clean you up before I drive you home.'

On the way it occurred to Hope that he could have driven her straight to the bungalow and have asked Barbara for brandy if he thought she needed it. And as if he read her thoughts, he said, 'It's a shade early for disturbing Barbara, and on principle I don't keep alcohol in the office. You weren't expecting that scene just now?'

'No. Nor that, when you arrived, you did seem almost to expect it. What did you mean when you said, "Why do we have this"—something I didn't understand—"every feast-day" and a few of the women laughed?'

He laughed shortly too. 'Ah, they understood the rest well enough. *Bef duva ka-bwe glo net*—patois for "The early bird gets the worm." They know that they don't *get* the worm—in other words the bonus, before their men claim it, but they always try it on, all the same.'

'You mean they've staged that mobbing of the *boucan* before?'

'Every time, and with the same result. Fortune coaxes them into the canteen, orders them coffee, dispenses a small gratuity to each of them, locks them in and only lets them out after the men have been paid.'

'A gratuity?' Hope puzzled. 'You give them money?'

'Of their own, to spend as they please.'

'But where does that appear on the pay-sheets?'

Craig's swift glance at her was oblique. 'Ever the scrupulous accountant! But don't worry. It doesn't have to. Our women workers are paid in the same way as the men, but these wives' sweeteners come from the privy purse.'

Hope thought that out. Then she asked boldly, 'From yours?'

'Where else? It's well worth it, since it serves to keep the peace——' As he spoke he was stopping the car and waiting for the approach of an old man with a face creased like a last year's pippin, tramping with the aid of a shoulder-high staff, who chuckled and replied smartly when Craig leaned out to speak to him in *patois*.

Craig drove on. 'That's Eli Caracas, our oldest employee,' he told Hope. 'I told him the wives were on the warpath again, and he snorted and said, "More fools, the men, for marrying them. I done fine all life without". Which is true,' Craig added. 'He lives alone on the estate; he doesn't know himself how old he is, but he never misses a day's work, though he hasn't too much stamina now.'

He drove under the porte-cochère and showed her into the living-room of his single-storey quarters in the courtyard of the Great House. He hooked a chair towards her, inviting her to sit down. Though she understood he had a daily help, she did not seem in evidence, and he himself fetched a bowl of disinfected hot water, adding lint and bandages from another journey, and brandy in a decanter from a cupboard.

At his orders Hope soaked her injured hand in the

bowl, while taking sips of the brandy from a glass in the other.

'Like it?' Craig asked casually.

She grimaced. 'It's warming, and it's better than whisky, which I hate. I'm beginning to like rum, as you drink it here, long, with lots of fruit juices and ice.'

'Well, tell yourself the brandy is only medicinal,' he advised. 'Show me that hand now.' He took it from the bowl, and laid it on the towel where again she could not control its violent trembling from wrist to fingertips. He looked up at her.

'What's the matter? Are you afraid I'm going to hurt you?'

She shook her head. 'No.'

'What then?'

She knew that it was at the expectation of his touch which she had guessed he would make gentle, but would be as coolly clinical as a doctor's. Her hand intimately in his meant nothing to him, and it mustn't to her. She made a painful fist of her fingers. 'It's nothing,' she said. 'Just shock.'

'Which is what the brandy was supposed to be in aid of. But as long as you don't suspect me of having lured you here in order to "take advantage" as the saying goes——'

'Of course not!' she denied hotly.

'In fact, nothing further from your thoughts.' Unfolding her fingers, he nodded at her blackened fingernails. 'You may be going to shed those,' he said, and when she agreed ruefully, he added, 'Found anything else to like about Madenina besides our rum punches?'

'Yes, a lot,' she told him.

He was dressing and bandaging each knuckle separately. 'What?'

'Well, I like my work here, and of course the climate——'

'Your cousin was badly disillusioned about that.'

'She expected too much.' Hope continued her list. 'And the people, and the different foods, and the gorgeous fruit. And the peace.'

'Hm, quite a detailed package—all in separate compartments. You don't, as most people would, make a cliché of it all—call it "the romance of the tropics" and let that say it all for them. Or doesn't your catalogue add up to anything as heady as romance? How do you find our men, for instance?'

'I've met very few of them.'

'Not? You don't seem to have lacked for them when you came to the Club.'

Lest that should lead to a mention of Luke Donat, Hope went on quickly, 'And Barbara doesn't entertain very much.'

'Not enough for you?'

'*Quite* enough for me. I'm very happy there,' she told him firmly, and as he had finished his work on her hand, she stood up. 'Thank you so much,' she said. 'It's marvellously comfortable now.'

'Good. But bathe it every day and get Barbara to renew the dressings.'

She flexed the fingers of her left hand. 'I may have to type with this one for a few days,' she warned.

'No problem. I can dictate to one of the juniors for the time being.'

He followed her out, but as he was about to put her into the car, Victoire de Faye was coming towards them from the house, and he waited for her.

Her glance at Hope was one of slightly critical enquiry. 'I wanted to see you,' she told Craig. 'But it looks as if, supposing I'd come a little earlier, I might have been interrupting something.'

'Nothing at all but a session in First Aid,' he replied evenly. 'Hope had a fall and I've been bandaging her fingers which she tore pretty badly.'

'Oh dear, I'm so sorry,' Victoire said in conventional concern. 'But don't you keep a First Aid cabinet at the office? You should.'

'So we do, but as I judged Hope could use a stimulant, I brought her here for cleaning up.'

'*And* for stimulation. I *see*.' The emphasis implied exactly the contrary. 'And now?'

'I'm driving her home. Why did you want to see me?'

'About the Friole merger. I have just heard from Emmanuel Friole that you have turned it down!'

Craig was opening the car door for Hope. 'That's so,' he agreed.

'You had no right!' Victoire flashed.

'I've only just clinched it. I had Hope make an abstract of the figures they furnished, and decided against.'

'Without consulting me?'

'I consulted you weeks ago—in late November,' he reminded her. 'I did nothing in haste, but I went ahead. Joining Belle Rose to a plantation like Friole might set everything going for them, but it could do nothing for us that we can't do better alone ...'

'So *you* claim you have the right to say!' she raged. 'But what am I on my own estate? A mere figurehead? A puppet, dancing to *your* pull on the string? No more than that, hm?'

Craig said, 'You know exactly where you stand in regard
to the estate, and if you'd wanted to argue the Friole
issue, I'd have talked it out with you at the time. But now
it's too late. They'll already be looking elsewhere for help
with their affairs, which is all they wanted from us. Meanwhile, you're fully at liberty to see the records which decided me. I'll have a copy of all the data sent over to you.'

Victoire made a gesture of distaste. 'You know very
well that figures mean nothing at all to me. I'd rather
trust my intuition and my flair, as most women do.' Then,
as if she regretted her outburst in front of Hope, whom it
had badly embarrassed, she said in a more conciliatory
tone, 'And so—*l'affaire* Friole beyond recall? Very well.
But there are one or two other things I'd like to take up
with you—*when*, of course, you feel free to attend to
them.'

'Matters—such as?'

'Eli Caracas, for one. He is nothing but a parasite
about the place. You must pay him off.'

Craig took his seat in the car. 'I'll do nothing of the
kind,' he said.

'Are you defying me?' Victoire demanded.

'In this instance, yes.'

'But he is occupying an estate cabin which should go to
a younger man. A married one, who would be worth his
pay. So if you are stubborn enough to keep Eli on, he
must move in with someone else, that's all.'

Craig said, 'No. Eli has been on the estate since he came
as a lad in your father-in-law's time. When Roland began
on the workers' quarters, he put Eli into the first to be
completed—the one-room affair he has still—and will
keep, while I remain manager.'

Victoire subjected him to a cold stare, her eyes hard.

'And *you* accuse *me* of making rights of my privileges! Who is presuming on his privileges now, may I ask?'

'The cases are different. I happen to have certain rights, as you very well know,' he said. 'What else did you want to say to me?'

'It can wait. Don't let me delay your errand of mercy any longer, *please*.' As Victoire turned on her heel Craig, apparently impervious to her gibes, said, 'I'll call at the house when I come back. Would Crispin like to come along for the ride?'

'Thank you, but Crispin has gone to the beach with his governess,' Victoire said loftily as she walked away.

Craig's only reference to the sharp exchange was to ask Hope to put the Friole papers on his desk on Monday. She, meanwhile, was thinking that she began to understand why Barbara had said that as an employer, he had no problems with his workers. Both this afternoon's happenings—his quixotic generosity to their wives and his championship of old Eli—showed he had a rapport with them which must make for their loyalty to him. Today he had shown himself in contradiction of the perfectionist she knew, and she found she was wondering what measure of his tolerance she could expect if she ever seriously failed him.

She remembered his edged criticism of her over Luke Donat—a lashing which she had thought made too much of her 'crime'. So did he keep his personal dealings in so many watertight compartments—one for his sympathy with his dependants, another for his impatience of ineptitude, another for his scorn of hearts-worn-upon sleeves, another for the tender understanding which for some reason he had lately withdrawn from Barbara? And did he ever allow any leakage from one compartment to another? Did he ever appear to be close and approachable, while remaining as remote as always? Just now, for instance, while his gentle care of her hand had only been that of a solicitous doctor's, his questions to her could have tempted her to believe in a curiosity about her which almost certainly he did not feel. No, there had been no leak of tenderness in her direction. The distance between them had not been cut.

The early evening shadows had begun to lengthen. Sundown was not yet, but was not far off. High above the horizon lay a long purple-black bank of cloud, its parallel lower edge as straight as if made by a ruler. Below it hung the crimson ball of the sun against the lemon-gold of a completely clear sky. Where trees grew along the roadside their upper branches made a filigree pattern against the backcloth of the sky, obscuring the view of the sinking sun until a break in the treeline laid the whole scene open again—cloud, sun, lemon sky, and the horizon lying in wait for the sun.

At one such point on the road Craig halted the car. 'Have you seen the green ray at sundown yet?' he asked.

Hope shook her head. 'I've never been so lucky,' she said.

'Then take your chance now.'

She sat forward eagerly. 'Could it happen this evening, do you think?'

'Maybe. Maybe not. But it has the makings of a sunset which might show it.'

'I do hope so! D'you think—if I stare and stare?'

'But not directly into the sun. Keep your eyes fixed on the point where it touches the horizon. You'll see nothing until the last tip of the rim is about to disappear. And then—green ray, or no green ray, according to your fate.'

'I'll watch.' He had not sat forward when she did, but she was conscious of his eyes upon her as he asked, 'What makes you so anxious to boast of having seen it?'

She remained face to the sun, not looking at him. 'Because Barbara says you can't count yourself as belonging here until you *have* seen it.'

'And that's your ambition? To belong in Madenina?'

'To—pretend I do, while I'm here. Of course I can't really.'

'You never know.' His tone was casual, lazy. 'Once over the green ray hurdle, you might take out naturalisation papers. Or we might marry you to a Madeninan-born. Either course would work it for you.'

She took time out from the sun to glance round at him and away again. 'You don't think I mean it, and perhaps I don't—as a permanency. But I think I'm in danger of being a little bewitched with the island. Or, if you would rather have it in a cliché, with "the romance of the tropics."'

'Throwing my words into my face? But they went home, did they? You admit to falling a victim, even though a reluctant one?'

'I haven't said I'm reluctant.'

'My mistake. I thought "bewitched" implied some conflict with your saner self; that you feel you should be above such tourist enthusiasms as, for instance, spotting the green ray.'

'Should I be so anxious to see it, if I were?'

'You could be—while you're under the spell, later to wonder why it all mattered to you. But keep looking. It won't be long now.'

The black mass of the cloudbank began to glow rosily and to break into drifting galleon shapes. When the top rim of the sun was only as narrowly crescent as a new moon, Craig spoke again.

'Even if the ray shows, it doesn't count if you're alone, you know,' he warned.

Not turning, 'It doesn't? Why not?' Hope asked.

'Obvious, surely? You need a witness to your claim of seeing it—a kind of guarantor. Didn't Barbara tell you?'

'No—— Oh! There it is ... was! I've seen it!' She turned to him, panting a little. 'It *was* there? You saw it too?'

'Yes. But describe it.'

'Well—at the very last moment there was this flash, as emerald green as—as—well, as emeralds,' she finished lamely.

'Good. Refer to me anyone who doubts that you've seen it. Meanwhile, my congratulations. But before you graduate as a true Madeninan, there is something else——'

'What?'

'Barbara should have told you. This——'

Side by side, they were very close, their thighs almost brushing. So that he had hardly to reach to draw her to him with one arm while tilting her chin between the forefinger and thumb of his other hand.

Then he kissed her—a long, masterful assertion by his lips upon hers, at first closed and unresponding from a surprise which came very near to shock, then pulsing in a hungry urgency which shook her to her depth.

But this was all wrong. They weren't lovers. He had no right! She had none—— She pulled free, feeling her colour mantle, seeking something to say which would conceal her hurt, and found it. She said unevenly, 'If—if that wasn't "taking advantage", I don't know what you would call it. It was utterly uncalled for and—and unforgivable.'

He sat back, regarding her gravely. 'Then you did suspect me of it?' he accused.

'Not then. Not for a moment. I thought you were being very kind. But——'

'But you found my kiss offensive?'

When she said nothing, he went on, 'Then you weren't listening to what I said. I told you there was another condition to your being accepted as one of us, through having seen the ray—and I demonstrated, without asking your permission. That's all.'

The chill in his tone had its sobering effect. She must *not* betray how his kissing her had stirred her craving for it to have meant more than it could have done. 'You mean,' she hesitated, 'that to be kissed by my—witness was a kind of forfeit I must pay to be believed?'

'Exactly. It confers a seal on your sighting of the ray.'

'You—you could have explained that,' she said lamely.

'And find myself graciously afforded the freedom of your cheek? I'm afraid I lost the habit of butterfly pecks about the time I left the nursery.'

That stung, goading her to retort, 'You still shouldn't risk your *apparent* enthusiasm being misunderstood, should you?'

He shrugged. 'Dare nothing, gain nothing.'

'Even though you weren't trying to gain anything—just carrying out a tradition, that was all?'

'Even though—never having seen enthusiasm as one of the more heinous crimes,' he said coolly as he switched on and drove off the grass verge where they had stopped. A few minutes later they reached the bungalow, and as

Hope thanked him and got out of the car she asked him if he were coming in.

He shook his head. 'No, I have to see Victoire. But tell Barbara, won't you, that you've taken your test and are now a fully paid-up member of the green ray union?'

Shaken, she remained standing where he left her, after he had driven away.

How could he? However conventional he claimed his kiss had been, did he really suppose she could go straight to Barbara who loved him, proclaiming that she had just come straight from being kissed by him? It was unthinkable, and she could only trust that she hadn't ever to admit to Barbara that she had seen the green ray and in whose company. As for herself, she could only blush inwardly at the thought of how nearly—how very nearly—she had been tempted to surrender to the seeming ardour of a kiss which had set her own desire afire.

How much had she allowed him to guess? How much had he known, and had despised her for it, and for her tardy acceptance of his not having meant anything more than a traditional gesture when he had kissed her?

If she had betrayed her need to him, what a fool he must think her! Nothing between them had led up to an emotional scene, and he had made painfully clear that nothing should lead away from it. 'Enthusiasm', he claimed, was all that had impelled him to kiss her as he had, and maintained that he saw no reason to deny it. So far as he was concerned, the incident was closed. And that had to go for her too, she realised bleakly, as she braced herself to go in to Barbara and to behave as if, since they last met, nothing had happened to set her world a-tilt and to spoil their relations through no fault of theirs.

CHAPTER SIX

BARBARA never now questioned Craig's failure to visit her, and this evening was no exception. She was full of sympathy for Hope's accident and showed she knew all about the wives' descent upon the *boucan* on the eve of every feast-day.

'And speaking of feast-days,' she said, 'Tina rang up to ask if she could bring Crispin here tomorrow while she goes to Jour de l'An with Luke Donat, and I said she could.'

'In the morning?' Hope asked.

'No, in the afternoon, and she'll collect him by sundown.'

'But you work in the afternoon.'

'Yes, well, I can always make time for Crispin.' Barbara hesitated before adding, 'I hadn't told you, but once or twice lately Tina has brought him here when she's wanted to have her hair done, or to do some shopping.'

'Doesn't she get time off for that kind of thing?'

'She says not, and that if Victoire does promise it to her, she's as likely as not to change her mind at the last minute.'

'I still don't think Tina should off-load Crispin on you when you want to work,' Hope claimed. 'But tomorrow I shall be here, and I can help you with him.'

'You aren't going to Jour de l'An yourself? I wouldn't suggest you go alone. It gets much too rowdy and one needs a man as escort, but I thought Craig might be taking you,' said Barbara.

Hope drew a sharp breath. 'Taking me? Why should he?'

Barbara shrugged. 'Just an idea, as it would be your first experience of a West Indian carnival. But there's always Mardi Gras, which is much more typically Madeninan, and you'll probably be invited to a party for that.'

Which sounded, Hope thought, as if, with Craig's defection, Barbara had opted out of any public appearances of her own. Why? True, she had introduced Hope to the Planters' Club, but that had been before her parting with Craig, and she had not suggested their going again. It was almost as if she were hiding from someone or something, though from what?

When, the next day, Hope suggested to Tina that she was making a convenience of Barbara, Tina was truculent, wanting to know why, since Barbara claimed to like having Crispin, she shouldn't be allowed to do just that.

Hope conceded, 'At times which suit her, why not? But why, just to help you out? And does Madame de Faye know you bring him here, while you go and do something else?'

'I don't tell her,' Tina admitted.

'Though he might.'

'I've risked that, and he hasn't yet. Anyway, if she won't give me time that I can call my own, she isn't entitled to know.'

'Even though,' Hope parried, 'you told me yourself that she and Barbara don't get on? So do you suppose she would care for his being here when she thinks he's in your charge?'

But Tina passed that off with a jaunty, '*I'm* not supposed to know they're at daggers drawn, and what the eye doesn't see——' and Hope had to leave it there.

Crispin, fortunately, was amenable to any suggestion made as to his amusement. He went for a walk with Hope; the three of them played paper games; he supervised the baking of scones for tea and contentedly listened to a story about pirates on the local radio.

He wanted to know how Hope had injured her hand and offered his own grubbily bandaged right thumb in a sympathetic gesture of misery-loves-company .

'You must learn to write with your left hand,' he advised. 'I can write with *my* left, if I have to.'

'Can you indeed?' admired Hope. 'Show me.'

'If you'll try too.'

Hope experimented, producing a shaky scrawl which earned only his grudging approval.

'I can do better than that,' he claimed, and did, concentrating hard with his tongue between his teeth. 'Belle-mère can write with *her* left too. That's what made me try, when I saw her doing it,' he remarked before he tired of the exercise and went on to something else.

The shadows began to lengthen, the sun was going down and Barbara began to be concerned for Crispin's homegoing. Tina had not yet come back for him, and presently even he mentioned with some satisfaction that in less than a quarter of an hour it would be his bedtime and he would miss it.

Barbara worried, 'It's too bad of Tina. I'll give her a little longer, but then I'd better drive Crispin home myself.'

They waited. No Tina. It was almost fully dark when Barbara decided to go, leaving Hope to guess how reluctantly she was going to beard Victoire on Victoire's own territory, and when she returned she was irate.

'Victoire was abominably rude,' she told Hope. 'She claimed she had no idea that Tina was out with Luke Donat, nor that Tina meant to leave Crispin with me, and wanted to know whether I really supposed she would countenance his being put in my charge—making an insult of the way she said '"your".'

'What did you say to that? asked Hope.

'I told her I resented her suggestion that he would be less safe with me than with Tina. At least I had brought him home more or less to time, which Tina hadn't.'

'And then?'

'She hadn't even the grace to thank me, implying that I was in league with Tina to deceive her, and I don't envy that one her reception when she does turn up at the House.'

When Tina did arrive nearly an hour later, she was full of apologies which Barbara brushed aside, saying that though she had seen Crispin safely home, she had no intention of being party to any such deception of Victoire in future. And Hope, on an intuition, asked Tina, 'Those other times when you left Crispin here, were you really going to the hairdresser's or into the town? Or were you keeping a date with Luke Donat then too?'

Tina's blue eyes threatened to fill. 'Then too,' she admitted. 'He's fun, and there was nowhere I could park Crispin but here. And now what am I to do? I've got to face Madame. Come with me?' she appealed to Hope. 'She has got nothing against you, and I daren't face her alone.'

Hope hesitated. 'There's nothing I can do.'

'Please!' Tina pleaded, and Barbara advised, 'You'd

better go, Hope. You may be able to serve as a buffer, even if Tina doesn't deserve one.'

'How do I get back?' Hope demurred.

'I'll follow you up in my car, and wait for you short of the house, which I am *not* visiting again while Victoire is mistress there,' Barbara declared with finality.

Tina and Hope found Victoire in the saloon. At sight of Tina her eyes flashed splinters of steel before the inevitable rain of accusatory questions began.

So? Tina had actually returned, had she? Where had she been? With whom? She had been engaged to take full charge of Crispin, hadn't she? Then what right had she to delegate his care to someone else—someone to whom she herself had no intention of owing the slightest obligation? How far *did* Tina suppose she was free to pursue her own pleasure at the child's expense? And how could she possibly hope to be trusted in future?

Even nearer to tears than she had been at the bungalow, Tina faltered in shamefaced reply, helped out by Hope when Victoire bullied her into incoherence. At last it was over. Victoire made a grievance of herself having seen Crispin to bed, sent Tina to the nursery under the threat of a suspended sentence of dismissal, and only when Tina had departed did she treat Hope as a guest and an equal.

'You will have an aperitif with me?' she invited, almost gracious now.

Hope declined, saying she had only come because Tina seemed afraid to come alone, that she mustn't take any more of Victoire's time, and that she hoped Victoire would be more lenient than Tina probably deserved.

'As to that, I shall have to see,' Victoire said rather cruelly. 'She has betrayed my trust in her, and that I do not easily forgive. But meanwhile, tell me about yourself, won't you?' With a glance at Hope's bandaged hand, 'Craig treated you kindly over that? You are not suffering with it too much? And you are reasonably contented with Barbara Paul as your landlady?'

'Very, thank you,' said Hope.

'And she entertains for you, I expect? You are getting to know some attentive young men?'

Hope answered that indirectly. 'No, Mrs Paul doesn't invite many people to her house. She's very busy most of the time, and I like a quiet life as much as she does.'

'Ah.' Victoire's slow nod added emphasis to the monosyllable. 'Though one hears that she is making a virtue of necessity—that she lives quietly because people do not visit *her*; not that she would not invite them if she thought they would accept.'

'Indeed?' said Hope, believing nothing of the kind. 'I must say I haven't that impression at all. I'm sure that why she doesn't entertain is because she chooses to live that way.'

'Yes, well, of course she must put the best face upon it,' Victoire conceded. 'She would not want you to know that she is not accepted as readily now as she and Nelson Paul were, when he was alive. But tell me—how often does Craig Napier visit her? Frequently? Not very often? Not at all?'

By now there was little doubt in Hope's mind that Victoire's questions were prompted by the malice she had towards Barbara. But how to answer this last one? Did she tell the truth—that Craig's very frequent visits had now dwindled to none; that she thought she could guess the reason was a lovers' quarrel? Or did she block Victoire's curiosity by saying she knew nothing of Craig's and Barbara's affairs? Or did she whet it, by claiming they were still as close as she had found them when she had come to the island?

What did Victoire want to hear? Suspecting she would welcome the news of their estrangement, Hope decided to imply the opposite. She said, 'I'm afraid I don't keep count of how often Mr Napier calls upon Mrs Paul. But I'm sure she values him as a friend, so I suppose they do meet fairly often.'

'Outside, you mean? They keep rendezvous?' asked Victoire sharply.

This Hope could answer frankly. 'I really don't know about that,' she said. 'But I suppose they see as much of each other as friends usually do.'

'And of course the word "friend" can cover as much or as little intimacy as people require of it, can it not?' Victoire insinuated, proving to Hope that she was being 'pumped' to some purpose and determining her to have no further part in it. She stood up, ignoring the question. 'I must go,' she said, but was not allowed to escape Victoire's final murmur, 'So *very* indiscreet of Craig to continue the association. But how can one ever advise a man in his own interest, if he is careless of it himself?' After which she allowed Hope to leave, showing no concern, however, as to how she was going back.

Barbara's greeting was an interested 'Well?' and when Hope recounted Tina's ordeal at Victoire's hands, she said, 'Well, the child had a lesson coming to her, but she didn't deserve scarifying like that. Will Victoire keep her on, do you suppose?'

'I don't know, though I should rather think so. Tina says she has very little time for Crispin herself. He hardly ever sees her, so if it weren't for Tina and the kitchen

staff, he would be left entirely on his own,' said Hope, letting Barbara suppose she had left straight after Tina's
despatch to the nursery, so that she hadn't to report on
Victoire's impertinent questions on Craig's relations with
Barbara.

It was odd, Hope thought wryly, how defensive and
protective of Barbara she felt, considering how she herself had been caught by Craig's magnetism. It was as if
loving the same man had forged a bond, rather than the
makings of jealousy, between them—a situation with its
own poignancy but no bitterness for the odd girl out—
herself. He had kissed her once with no more meaning
than would be asked of him in a game of Forfeits. He had
kissed Barbara in loving solicitude many times and, whatever their present difference, no doubt he would kiss her
in love again. And because Barbara was Barbara—kind,
courageous and full of character—the odd girl out could
envy her but could not hate.

It was with a good deal of diffidence that Hope met Craig
at the office that Monday following the Jour de l'An. But
he was so much his imperious self, rapping out orders
and expecting swift compliance, that it was easy to conclude he had completely dismissed the possibility that he
had embarrassed her on Friday night.

As always during the weeks she had worked for him,
she marvelled at the range of the responsibility he carried
and the expertise with which he dealt with the problems it
brought. On that one day he was office executive and appeal court; he was called out to one of the plantations on
a suspected case of pest infestation in a young crop; on
this post-holiday Monday he had also to adjudicate in the
case of a plantation worker who, 'high' on weekend rum,

had attacked his mate with a cane-cutlass—all this between dealing with his correspondence and frequent telephone calls to and from the communal sugar-mills.

He was at his desk when the postal clerk brought in the afternoon mail, to be sorted by Hope for anything she could handle on her own initiative, the rest to be passed to him for his comment and ruling. Today most of it was trivial, the only other letter being an airmail from the Netfold and Islay Head Office which she carried to Craig unopened.

He glanced through it, then up at her. 'Had you heard anything like this was afoot?' he asked.

'Anything of which?'

'Read it.' He passed the letter to her and waited for her comment.

'This publicity scheme for a television documentary on sugar? No,' she told him. 'There was no mention of it before I left England.'

'And how do you view the idea?'

'I?' She looked her surprise at the question.

'Well, should we co-operate or not?'

She shook her head. 'How should I know? Isn't it for Madame de Faye and you to decide?'

'For me to decide. For Victoire to acquiesce. And I wasn't asking for your expert advice, but to speak for the average English woman viewer who uses sugar. Would she welcome a programme as to where her coffee-crystals and her molasses begin?'

'I think she would. I don't remember ever seeing one about cane.' Hope referred back to the letter. 'I gather Publicity proposes to approach TV; they send out a team to film the whole process here on Belle Rose?'

Craig nodded. 'From the cane roots up, you could say.'

He took back the letter and re-read it himself. He fingered his chin in thought. 'Yes ... yes. Come March, they can film the spring *ratoon* which should be sizeable, and beforehand we can school them on everything else. Yes, I think we should play along.' He tapped the paper with a fingernail. 'This signature—this Perse—Publicity and Public Relations. He's been over here twice, though we didn't meet. I was in Barbados. A bit of a youngling, I believe—do you know him yourself?'

'Yes. He *is* young, but they think a lot of him at Head Office,' said Hope, with a memory of Ian, of his slightly diffident courting and of the Happy Landings posy which had faded so soon.

'Well?'

The crisp question, cutting into her thoughts, sounded irrelevant. 'Well? Well what?' she echoed lamely.

'I was asking whether you knew Perse well, and if so, how well?' Craig pointed out. 'In what sort of connection have you met him? Socially or on a business level or how?'

'Oh, I see! Well, socially mostly. We've played tennis together and been to Head Office functions—dances and things. He's been to my uncle's house too.'

'Married?'

'No.'

'And business-wise?'

'I've told you—he has a good reputation with the Directors. Why, if you do invite the TV team, do you think he means to come out too?'

'Well, don't you?' Craig parried. 'If the idea is his baby, do you suppose he'll let it be nursed along without his foot on the cradle-rockers? No, it sounds to me as if he's inviting himself, so you'll be able to continue your acquaintance, won't you?'

'We can do that when I go home again,' Hope said evenly.

'You can count on his still being available when you do go?'

'Available?'

'To partner you at tennis and to escort you to dances? Or, as a Coming Man with a Future, does he never give you cause to fear competition for him?'

Where was this catechism leading? 'I've never thought about it,' she said.

Craig laughed shortly. 'Does that mean modesty forbids your admitting you have never *had* to think about it? Well, all right, we'll invite him, and I must resist the temptation to suspect that his astute timing has anything to do with the slaughter of two birds with one stone.'

Hope tried to work that out. 'Are you implying that he's coming because he wants to see me?'

'The thought had occurred.'

'Well, it needn't!'

'No?' That was all. Glancing at her injured hand, in his next breath he was asking her to call a junior to take the dictation of his reply to Ian's letter. He had become the unapproachable autocrat once more.

It seemed that Hope had been right in thinking that Victoire would conveniently overlook Tina's truancy, for Tina, at least outwardly contrite, was soon returned to the favour of her employer's whims.

Nominally she was given the freedom of one afternoon a week, and when this did not clash with Victoire's convenience she had the use of the runabout car to take her where she pleased.

It was on one such ticket-of-leave Saturday that she met Barbara and Hope shopping in the town. They had tea at

a café and exchanged news. Tina had received her
mother's approval and a sizeable cheque from her father,
enabling her to stay on in Madenina until he sent her the
next; Hope told her of the proposed television project and
that Ian Perse was to escort the team.

'Fun for you,' commented Tina. 'You'll have someone
to to go around with at last.' She explained to Barbara,
'This Ian character fancies Hope no end. I wouldn't put it
past him to have laid this on, so that he could get out to
see her. When do they come?' she asked Hope, who said,

'They're due by the banana ship in about ten days.
And if you suppose Ian has all that influence with the
Top Table, you'd better think again.' She was irritated
that Tina should have jumped to the same false conclusions as Craig had. Ian was coming and it was logical
that he should. But for her he had become so shadowy
and unimportant a figure that she knew she wasn't looking forward to his appearance on the Madenina scene.

Presently Barbara excused herself. There was no house
delivery of mail on the island, and she wanted to collect
her letters from her Post Office box.

'I'll come with you,' Hope offered.

'No. No, I'll bring any mail there may be for you. But
stay with Tina, and I'll call back for you,' said Barbara.

Looking after her as she went out into the street, Tina
mused, 'Easy to guess why she didn't want you along.'

'Didn't want me? What do you mean?' Hope asked.

'That she isn't likely to want anyone along when she
collects her letters. For instance, have you ever been with
her lately when she's called for them—or opened them?'

'I don't know that I have. But what are you hinting at,
for goodness' sake? That Barbara has something to
hide?'

Tina nodded. 'Something *I'd* want to hide—anony-mous letters. Well, wouldn't you?'

Hope stared. 'Anonymous letters? To *Barbara*? How on earth do you know?'

'From Madame de Faye.'

'And how should *she* know?'

'I suppose she has her spies. Barbara is very far from being one of her favourite people, and I'd say that Bar-bara in trouble would just about make her day.'

'But what kind of trouble could Barbara be in that Vic-toire de Faye would know about?' worried Hope.

'I'm not saying she knows *what* trouble,' Tina corrected. 'Only that she isn't sorry about the letters she hears Bar-bara has been getting, and the reason for that's pretty obvious. It's—Craig.'

'*Craig?*' But Hope was not as incredulous as her echo sounded, realising as she did now that Victoire's pointed questions about Craig's intimacy with Barbara had only been part of a pattern of hostility to which Tina had just added another piece.

Victoire, all her knives out against Barbara, was pre-pared to sharpen them where she could—on the welcome news that Barbara had an anonymous enemy; on what-ever she had tried to trick Hope into revealing about Craig's and Barbara's association. But what she did hate about it? What had she, the wealthy owner of Belle Rose, to fear from it? Though despising her curiosity, Hope re-peated with less emphasis, 'Craig Napier? How do you mean he's involved?'

'In the usual way,' said Tina airily. 'Madame is jealous of Barbara Paul—plain, green-eyed jealous, that's what. Ever heard it makes enemies of people, no?'

So! For Hope it was as if another shape in the ugly

design had dropped into place. Victoire hated Barbara because she wanted Craig herself! And yet how could she, when at every turn that Hope had witnessed, she and Craig seemed to be fighting for mastery, the one over the other, Craig's dynamism winning against Victoire's worst possible grace. No cordiality, no pulling together, no friendship, no willing surrender ... No, it just wasn't possible. Tina and the pattern *had* to be wrong!

But perhaps it was to convince herself as much as Tina that she said, 'Of course. But I don't believe it of Craig and Victoire. They don't seem even normally friendly.'

'Do they have to be, in front of other people?' Tina countered. 'What did I tell you about the love-hate thing? She probably provokes him deliberately because she enjoys being bullied by him. And can he bully? Oh, my!'

Hope did not reply, but she looked at Barbara with a new curiosity when the latter returned, bringing two letters for Hope, but saying nothing of having found any awaiting herself, until Tina asked pertly, 'No luck? Too bad,' to which Barbara said, 'Yes, there was one for me. Nothing important,' in a flat tone which could have been either casual or snubbing. If Tina's guess were right, there was nothing in Barbara's manner to confirm it, and Hope could not know then how errant chance was to give Barbara's secret into her own reluctant hands.

One of her letters was from Ian Perse, written from England before he and the television crew had left for Madenina by sea. He wrote eagerly. It had been too long since he had seen her; her news of Madenina, of the 'Wish you were here' variety, wasn't enough. By the time she got his letter, it wouldn't be long before he arrived himself; she had better see to it that she kept her job with Craig Napier until then; it wouldn't be at all funny if he landed on Madenina to find she was on her way back to England; meanwhile he could hardly wait.

Hope read this on the verandah when she and Barbara had returned to the bungalow that evening. Barbara, who had been in her room earlier but was not there now, had left wide her french window on to the verandah, and as Hope was refolding Ian's letter, reflecting that he was taking a lot for granted, a sudden gust of wind swept some small litter—a dressing-table mat, a tissue, a folded paper—out from the room to flutter at Hope's feet.

She picked them up, her thumb inadvertently uncreasing the paper as she did so. There was some writing on it —not Barbara's, but an awkward, disjointed scrawl of a few words which forced themselves upon the eyes.

She read,

'One trusts you are learning your lesson—that soon you will have no friends at all, if you continue to encourage your lover. And though you may care nothing for your own already damaged reputation, one would suppose that you might care about his.'.

That was all. It was without greeting or signature, and though she had never seen one before, Hope knew it at once for what it was—a piece of cowardly scurrility which had to be sent under disguise. But even without Tina's hints, Hope would have been in little doubt that the recipient was Barbara; it had been swept from her room, and whether or not it had arrived today, she must have received it, opened it and read it at some time.

Nor could Hope wonder as to the 'lover' to whom it referred. Sick with dismay, she knew—even without Tina's help—that it was Craig. Craig—who hadn't been near Barbara unnecessarily for weeks, but the same Craig who had once been her welcome, near-daily visitor; who had often kissed her, and on one night Hope remembered only too well, had held her in his arms—but had not willingly met her again since.

Craig—who had left her to engage in some kind of grotesque travesty of a love-affair with Victoire de Faye? *Craig*?

Hope fingered the letter she held. It wasn't hers. She shouldn't have read it, however boldly the bizarre script had demanded her curiosity. In her other hand were the lace mat and the tissue. She must put them all back, close the window upon them and for all her pity and bewilderment, must keep the happening from Barbara.

But as she moved towards the window a thought struck her about the letter's wording.

'One trusts'. 'One would suppose', it had said—a usage which was much more common to French than to English. So who, of the few people in Barbara's circle, was French? It had to be a woman. Poison-pen writers always were—*A woman*?

Suddenly, on a totally unreasoned flash of intuition, Hope was sure she knew who the writer was; that it was no vague enemy of Barbara's; it was a very certain one, Victoire de Faye herself!

It was something Hope felt she knew as surely as if Victoire had admitted it, knew it both by instinct and by an as tiny, trivial a memory as she had ever experienced—Crispin's innocent, 'Belle-mère can write with her left hand too. That's what made me try, when I saw her doing it.'

To Hope's mind it proved that Barbara hadn't two enemies, but only one; the one who, however warpedly, wanted Craig Napier; who hadn't known, when she had questioned Hope, how far she had succeeded in wresting

him from Barbara, and had continued to use the means
by which she meant to do it.

And in all this coil, what prospects were there for Hope
herself? None, obviously, but that of being for Craig the
robot he had claimed he would welcome as a work-
partner. When she went back to England he would have
already forgotten that he had ever kissed her lightly
in the name of an island tradition; he would remember
her only as the girl who had heeded his warning that efficient secretaries shouldn't harbour sentimental dreams.

CHAPTER SEVEN

I<small>F</small> only, Hope thought, Barbara would confide in her! Though if Barbara had no more proof of Victoire's authorship of the letters than she herself had, and if she feared that Craig had indeed deserted her for Victoire, she might be reluctant to move against her rival for Craig's sake. For even Hope could see that such a scandal would have the recoil of a whip. Belle Rose would suffer, and so might Craig, and Hope's guess was that Barbara's generosity would not invite that.

But where was it all going to end? What had Barbara done—or been—that could give Victoire grounds for her threats of Barbara's continuing ostracism by her friends? And what was the real truth of that? *Was* Barbara being deliberately shunned? Hope felt it was more than possible that she would never know.

Now, with the onset of spring, work all over the plantation was quickening. On new land the cuttings which had rooted during the winter rains were sprouting into vigorous growth, were being fertilised, sprayed with insecticides and weeded, though not scheduled for harvesting until the maturity of their first *ratoon*, twelve months or so ahead.

On established terrain the previous year's cuttings were being readied for their own first *ratoon*, as were longer-established canes for their second and third and the rest of their productive life. Here the overall scene was of a forest of stout stems, broad branching greenery, topped by feathery fronds as soft to the touch as pampas grass and as decorative.

There were alarms, false and genuine, of pest infestations, unseasonal floods, and prophecies of a sugar market from which the bottom had fallen out. In the office, tables of incentive bonuses—for working in heavy wet undergrowth or on the unpopular days of the weekend— were drawn up, to be rejected by the foremen, returned for revision and finally agreed with the management. A system of patrols was set up to guard the ripened canes from theft by the neighbourhood children in search of a sweetmeat, and by their parents, well practised in the art of putting pirated cane through the family mangle to extract a rough intoxicant from the sugar juice. And in the midst of all this heightened activity on Belle Rose the banana ship, on its fortnightly shuttle between England and the banana-producing islands of the West Indies, docked in Port Belain harbour.

Victoire, flattered by the publicity Belle Rose would collect to the envy of the other local estates, was graciously laying on a party for the television team and the captain and officers of the ship on its overnight stay in port. Hope was invited, but Barbara was not, and if Hope had been able to think of a plausible excuse she would not have accepted for herself. But Craig took it for granted she would go, both to the party and to meet the ship with him at the docks.

They drove down. They were early and the ship was not in. But the usual gay crowds which gathered for the periodic excitement of 'banana ship day' were already there, milling up and down in festive idleness; tourists with cameras at the ready, pedlars touting fruit and souvenirs and West Indian girls, rainbow-dressed on flirtation parade, going into huddles of giggling feminine gossip and too-pointedly ignoring the ogling men and boys of their set, as leisured and sauntering as themselves.

Craig installed Hope at a table on the front terrace of the Yacht Club, brought her the drink she chose and joined her with his own.

They watched the kaleidoscope scene on the quays. Hope, admiring the girls' gay dresses, hadn't understood Craig's comment on the jaunty flair of their headkerchiefs.

'The one-points and the fours well in the majority, but that's to be expected, the twos and threes having no further need to advertise,' he had said, and to her puzzled look, 'Has nobody explained to you the code of signals they use by the way they tie the *madras*—that gaudy bit of nonsense on their heads?'

'Signals? To whom?' Hope queried.

'To the men, of course, as to their availability. For instance—one corner of the *madras* tweaked upright means the girl is heartwhole and unattached. A show of two points means she's engaged; three, that she's happily married, and four, that though she may be married or a young widow, she doesn't want it thought she's out of the hunt for good. It's a variation on the invitation-game all women play—a shade more direct, that's all.'

Hope sat forward, counting perky knottings in proof, and finding it. 'And does it get them the man they want, do you suppose?' she asked.

'A particular one? Who knows? But at least they're offering him a short cut, while being fair to all the others.' Craig paused. 'I hear from Victoire there's a little woman in a boutique on Nassau Boulevard who ties a very chic *madras* for her clients. On fancy-dress occasions Victoire has worn one herself with considerable panache. If you're interested, I daresay the lady would run one up for you too.'

Hope shook her head. 'I don't think it's quite my style.'

'As a headdress or a green light of invitation—which?'

She ignored the provocation in the question. 'As a headdress, naturally. An English girl would look absurd wearing one.' In an effort to restore whimsy to a subject which he seemed determined to make personal, she added, 'Anyway, why should the girls have to do the inviting? And why isn't there a points system for the ones who are quite happy to wait until a man shows he's attracted to *them*?'

'In answer to your first question—Because they enjoy the open competition, and because it lends them power. And to your second—Because, in the words of the classics, "There ain't no sich animal".'

'And that's your experience—that there are no women who aren't concentrating heavily on getting a man or preening themselves for having got one?' she suggested lightly.

A nod. 'That's my experience,' he confirmed.

'Without any exceptions?'

'No more than go to prove the rule. And they'd be freaks of nature.'

'Which makes you something of a cynic, don't you think?'

' "Cynic" I deny. A realist—yes.' At some increased bustle on the quay he stood up and drained his glass. 'It looks as if there's about to be some action,' he said. 'Let's go down.'

On their way, at the foot of some steps, their passage was blocked by a West Indian youth, camera in hand.

With a wide grin he flattered Craig, 'Mister, how come you get pretty gal widout she wear one-point to tell she willing?'

Craig threw Hope an amused glance. 'This is where we came in,' he murmured, and told the youth, 'Man, it takes personal magnetism, what else?'

The boy shook his head in non-comprehension. 'You make mock wid long words, mister. But I take picture and you pay—yes?' He brandished the camera, a polaroid. 'See—picture instan'. No wait. No come-out, no pay. Yes?'

'Oh, very well.'

But after taking their range through the viewfinder, the youth lowered the camera. 'Love-pose better,' he observed. 'Charge no more. Make better picture, that' all.'

Craig sighed resignedly, moved a step nearer to Hope and put his arm round her, ignoring her quiver of surprise. 'That do, man?' he asked.

A grudging nod appeared to acknowledge that it would have to, and the picture was taken. 'Two minutes. Three. Picture come. You see!'

But it didn't, and they didn't. Peeled free, the film was as blank as a foggy night, and the enraged owner shook the camera in horrified disgust. 'Man sell it cheap, he say perfec'. Make good money wid. *Good money*—huh!' he fulminated. 'I been done!'

Craig released Hope and took money from his trouser-pocket. 'Never mind, man. These things happen,' he said. 'How much?'

The glowerings turned to an astonished but radiant smile. 'You still pay, mister? No picture, but you pay?'

'If it had come out, it would have been worth it,' said Craig cryptically. 'And the camera? Bought it from a man in the street, I daresay? How much?'

'Fifteen dollars.'

'Then here—and don't sell it for twenty to the next mug who comes along,' Craig warned, adding paper money to the coins in his hand and handing them over. He turned back to Hope and as they walked on, 'A pity, that,' he said. 'But I daresay you're relieved. A "love-pose" for you and me not quite in order in the circumstances, you were thinking, hm?'

In fact, she was intrigued and warmed by a quixotry which was all of a piece with his generosity to his workers' wives. She was wondering what would have been the fate of the snapshot if it had come out. Would he have discarded it as a piece of nonsense? Would he have kept it? Or handed it over to her? And she was wishing she could say all this to him with ease. But because she couldn't, she ignored his question, to which he probably hadn't expected an answer anyway.

An hour later the graceful white ship had docked and its small complement of passengers was coming off. The TV team consisted of half a dozen men whom Ian Perse introduced to Craig by their names and various functions. Then he saw Hope standing in the background and went to greet her eagerly, taking both her hands in his and kissing her. Light and friendly as the kiss was, she flinched from it slightly, hoping Craig hadn't noticed, lest he chose to read into it an intimacy with Ian which she had been at so much trouble to deny.

Craig had ordered a couple of hire-cars for the visitors, in which they drove off to their hotel after accepting his invitation to Victoire's party and making an appointment to survey the estate the next morning, preparatory to their first shootings of film. While Craig had gone on board to extend Victoire's hospitality to the Captain, Ian had drawn Hope aside.

'I'll leave these cars to the boys and hire one of my own. May I call for you to take you to this affair tonight? How do I find you?' he asked.

Glad that she hadn't to be obliged to Craig to take her, she had directed Ian to the bungalow, and he had left with the others before Craig returned to his own car where she was waiting for him.

'Threads taken up where you and Perse had dropped them?' he asked casually on the way back to the office.

'As far as there were any to pick up, yes,' she said.

'By his welcome he appeared to think there were some. Did he suggest escorting you to Victoire's party tonight?'

'Yes, he's calling for me.'

'Losing no time, evidently,' was Craig's comment.

At that she turned on him, goaded. 'I can't think why you insist on reading so much into my friendship with Ian Perse,' she said. 'From what I've told you about my knowing him, and from the little you've seen of us together, why do you assume that we're more than friends?'

'Because I don't believe in freaks of nature. Since, on the available evidence, you're neither engaged, nor married, nor a merry widow, you must be what's known locally as a "one-point gal".'

'Signalling my willingness to Ian Perse?'

'Why not? And short of having surprised your eyes lighting with invitation to any other man, one can be excused for jumping to conclusions. Are you going to confess to him that you've been kissed against your will since the two of you last met?'

The utter inconsequence of the question took Hope aback. 'Of course not,' she denied. 'And I wasn't——'

'—Weren't unwilling? Oh, come! The Ice Maiden *par excellence*, you!'

She blushed furiously. 'I meant I wasn't kissed like—like that. It was just the—the customary thing. You said so!'

'So Perse isn't to be told? Ah well, you'll have to see that he spots the green in the sunset while he's here, and you can level scores in that way, can't you?' Craig taunted unanswerably, and Hope attempted no reply.

In view of the party he suggested later that she should leave the office early, and, back at the bungalow, she was having a drink with Barbara after dressing when a car drew up outside.

'That must be Ian, though he's before his time,' said Hope. But it wasn't Ian to whom Barbara opened. It was Tina, white-faced and panting, who broke past her.

'You've got to help, you've got to do something!' she clamoured. 'Hope——! Barbara, *please*! I can't—I don't know what——' She broke off, a fist at her mouth, her eyes wide.

Barbara took her firmly by the arm. Hope went over to her.

'What's happened?'

'What's the matter?'

Their voices had clashed. Tina gulped. She was shaking all over now. 'It—it's Crispin,' she stammered. 'In the car—He's ill——'

'Ill? How? Car-sick? Or what?' Barbara demanded while Hope ordered, 'Tina! Pull yourself together! And if Crispin is ill, why did you leave him? Why didn't you bring him in?'

'Because—because she said I wasn't to—ever.'

'Because *who* said?'

'She means Victoire, of course.'

Hope's questions and Barbara's explanation had clashed again. Then Barbara was out of the door, and Tina was whimpering, 'That's right. Madame said I was never to bring him here again. And I wouldn't have, only —only I daren't take him home,' she finished as Barbara returned with the little boy, whose own hand was at his throat.

'He can't speak,' Barbara announced tersely.

'I—I know,' Tina admitted. 'He can hardly open his mouth, but I could just see that inside it's all—sort of ulcerated and—and dry.'

'But how come? Where have you been? What has he been doing? How could he start an ulcerated mouth— suddenly, just like that?'

Both girls' questions tumbled over each other, and Tina answered in staccato. 'I've been out with Luke. It's my afternoon off. We left my car and went for a drive in his. And Crispin stayed to play on the beach——'

'What beach?'

'Cloud's Nest. It's perfectly safe. No tide to come in and nobody about. He didn't mind being left. We went on—to Witch Creek and had a swim, and then—well, round about. Maybe we were away a bit long, but—— And then, on the way back, a little short of Cloud's Nest, there was a car parked, with some friends of Madame's. And as they might tell her I had been out with Luke without Crispin, I made him stop and let me get out to leave the road and cut across the sands on foot to where I had left Crispin. And—and this was how I found him. His hands too—they're blistered. Look——'

Barbara had already looked, when he had flinched at her gentle touch. And as Tina faltered, 'Could he have been poisoned or—or anything?' it was as if the same thought struck the other two at the same moment.

Remembering Luke Donat's warning, Hope murmured aloud, 'Cloud's Nest? There's a tree there that's poisonous, the fruit and the leaves——' and Barbara confirmed,

'Yes, the manchineel,' and knelt to level herself with Crispin. 'Darling, just nod for Yes or shake your head for No,' she urged. 'Did you eat or taste anything while Tina was away? Or even just play under one of the big trees there are up the beach at Cloud's Nest Bay?'

A nod answered her.

'Perhaps you bit into the fruit—like small pippins—which were on the tree, or some that had fallen?'

Another nod, and a grimace twisted his mouth. Barbara stood up and turned on Tina. 'He has been poisoned—in a way. Had no one warned you about the manchineel—how it dries up saliva and blocks the throat? Hadn't Madame de Faye warned you against it?'

Tina shook her head wretchedly. 'I've never heard of it. How did *you* know about it?' she demanded of Hope.

'Luke Donat told me.'

Tina frowned suspiciously. '*Luke*? *You've* been with him to Cloud's Nest?'

'Not with him. He arrived there once when I was just leaving.'

'Oh——' Tina's attention was diverted by the sight of Barbara wrapping Crispin in a blanket. 'What are you doing?' she asked.

'Guarding against shock.'

'You mean I've got to take him home like that? But I can't! I daren't!'

'He's not going home. But *you* are,' Barbara ordered. 'He's going to hospital——'

'To hospital? What for? What will they do to him there?'

'I don't know. I've heard of manchineel poisoning, but I've never seen a case of it. It could mean a tracheotomy —I don't know. Meanwhile, you're going back to the House, to tell Victoire all about it, and where she can find Crispin within the next half hour.'

'I can't! I can't! She'll never forgive me!' Tina whimpered, close to hysteria.

'Never is a long time. But for the moment you can hardly expect a pat on the head,' Barbara told her brutally as Hope went to answer the door to Ian, keeping his date with her.

She explained the crisis to him. 'I can't come with you,' she told him.

'But you're dressed! Ready——!'

'I know. But I can't leave Barbara to take Crispin to hospital alone. You must go, though if there'll be any party when Madame de Faye hears what Tina has to tell her, one can't tell.' As a thought struck her, she appealed to Tina, 'Will you go and face Madame if Ian goes with you? Because you do realise that Barbara is right—you must go?'

Reluctant and protesting, Tina consented to being pushed out and into Ian's hired car. When they had gone Barbara went to get her own car, and with Crispin in the back seat, supported by Hope, they drove into town.

At the hospital soft, concerned West Indian voices greeted them and compassionate hands and skills took over. The two girls waited for news, and waited, expecting Victoire's arrival at any minute.

But time passed and she did not come. She had surely telephoned? Barbara asked. No, there had been no call from Madame de Faye. And she had neither rung nor appeared when they were joined in their waiting by Craig. Craig alone.

Whatever the rift between them, his greeting to Barbara was his outstretched hand. She took it and clung to it as he asked of Crispin, 'How is he? Have you heard?'

'They think they needn't operate; that they can treat him conservatively with drugs,' she told him. 'That's all, up to now. But where is Victoire? Tina did make her understand?'

'She isn't coming. She didn't think it was necessary.'

'Didn't ... think ... it ... was ... necessary!' Barbara's slow, incredulous echo almost spelled out each word and Hope protested,

'But why not? Why couldn't she come? If she had to put off Ian and the TV team, they would surely have understood?'

'It wasn't a case of excusing herself to them, but to at least fifty other people.' Craig's tone was flat, unemotional; he was making a report on Victoire, showing nothing of approval or censure. 'She had invited everyone in the island who counts, from the Prefect and the Mayor downward, and she couldn't feel justified in disappointing them by calling off the party——'

'Even though Crispin might have died? Might still?'

'Considering all things, Victoire decided she needn't come.'

'So she sent you instead? As—as her lackey?' There

was a world of scorn in Barbara's voice and Hope held her breath, waiting for his answer.

He said tautly, 'Victoire "sends" me nowhere; no woman does.' He had relinquished Barbara's hand and he now turned to Hope.

'When did you last have a report? And where is Crispin?'

She told him and he went to see what he could learn from the staff. When he came back he said there was no point in their staying longer. Crispin had been treated and sedated, was now sleeping and could probably go home in a couple of days. To Hope's surprise Craig took it for granted that he would be taking her on to the party, and when she demurred he insisted that she put in an appearance as one of his staff and as Victoire's guest. Barbara agreed that he was right. 'Victoire has nothing to blame *you* for, and you did rather make use of your young man, making him a bodyguard for Tina,' she said, and that she was fully prepared to go home alone.

They parted outside the hospital, though Craig escorted Barbara's car as far as the bungalow, before driving on to the Great House.

On the way Hope asked him what would happen to Tina after this latest breach of duty, adding that it was hardly to be expected that Victoire would be willing to keep her on as Crispin's governess.

'If she doesn't, will she engage another for him, or will he go back to school?' she asked.

'That remains to be seen,' said Craig. 'Keeping him on the island after his Christmas holidays was by way of an experiment, and when he's recovered from this lot, I'll look at the situation again.'

Hope wondered if she had misheard his use of 'I', and

he appeared to sense from her silence that she was puzzled.

'Roland de Faye made me Crispin's full guardian,' he explained. 'You'd expected that Victoire, as his stepmother, would have that capacity?'

'Well, naturally.'

'And naturally I consult her about him. But where his future is concerned, as the Americans say, the buck stops with me.'

'So that it's for you to say whether Tina stays or goes?'

'Not altogether. I'll fall in with Victoire's wishes on that. But I think you'd agree that in both her roles out here, Tina hasn't been an unqualified success?'

Metaphorically Hope backed away. 'It's hardly fair to ask me that,' she said.

'Which means you agree. How far is she involved now with Donat, do you know?'

'Only that she's been seeing him quite often.'

'She's a silly child. He's known for being the island's Don Juan. Which reminds me—when did you realise that yourself for your own good?'

Hope retorted sharply, 'I never was under any illusions about him.'

'No? I seem to remember your being pretty aggrieved when I took you to task for wasting your—and my—time with him.'

'My being late that day wasn't my fault, as I tried to tell you. He'd tricked me into it, by bribing a boy to take my scooter for a joyride, guessing he could make trouble for me with you.'

'Why should he want to do that?'

'Because I'd given him the brush-off at the Planters' Club, and when I sent him back to Tina, he told me I was a schoolmarm, or words to that effect. So when you refused to let me explain, I felt I had reason to be aggrieved, and I'm afraid I showed it.' She blushed at the memory.

'You did,' Craig agreed. 'In fact, you were insufferably rude, and I don't excuse the strong-arm tactics I felt you'd earned, though perhaps I've learned better since.'

'Better?'

'Learned you better—that fishwife snarlings aren't your usual line; that you're not a Tina; you're not cut from the kind of flimsy that a Luke Donat can work on, and no wonder you baffled him and enraged him with your self-possession and your general *sang-froid*. On occasion, I've been at the receiving end of it myself.'

Hope drew a long breath. Then, resolved to daring, she said, 'In other words, he read me rightly for what I am? A—how did it go?—a "plain jane with her head screwed on"?'

He laughed with a harsh sound. 'And how did you hear about that?'

'From Barbara.'

'I might have known. But be fair—didn't she report too that I liked your voice?'

'Yes.'

'And was that such a bad evaluation, merely by telephone?'

'I suppose not. But you don't deny that I do give people the impression that I'm the no-nonsense, schoolmarm type?'

He appeared to consider that. Then he said, 'I think I prefer my estimate of this morning—that if you insist you're not wearing your one-point for Perse, you're probably the sublime Ice Maiden—hidden fires notional, but not guaranteed. How about that?'

'As a flight of fancy, fine,' she agreed. 'But as a description of me—well, who would care for being thought—frigid?'

'Not even with hints of possible arousal? I'd have thought that, compared with two-a-penny schoolmarms and plain janes, Ice Maidenhood might have an appeal as rarity value. But it hasn't?'

'No.'

'Sorry. My mistake.'

But as that was no apology, but the kind of thing people said while remaining convinced they were right, Hope thought it time to change the subject, if he would let her. But when, after a small silence, she said on impulse, 'I'm worried about Barbara; she's not at all the sunny person she was when I first came here,' as soon as the words were out, she realised she had probably invited a snub.

As she had. She watched his lips compress to a hard line. 'And do you think I don't know it?' he said.

She hesitated. 'I thought you must, but that you might know the cause and be able to help her. I—I'm sorry.'

'And supposing that, as things are, I can't help her?'

'Then I shouldn't have brought it up, and there's nothing more to be said, is there?' she retorted. And when he agreed, 'Nothing, I'm afraid,' she felt he had confirmed that he *had* thrown Barbara over.

That close embrace between them on the last of his almost daily visits to the bungalow must have been wrung from him by Barbara, and even on leaving her he hadn't been able to refuse it. That night, Hope felt sure, she had been the unwilling witness of a parting which had been one of Barbara's willing, and the thought was almost a physical pain.

For like Barbara, she had allowed herself to love the man at her side, and though he wouldn't ever know it, she felt ashamed that she had let it happen. 'Feet of clay'. The phrase sprang to her mind and wouldn't be quieted in relation to Craig. For respect and admiration mattered in love. It was abject to love blindly without them, and Craig's callous admission that he could do nothing for Barbara had destroyed them for her. At that moment Hope almost wished she could hate him. But she could not—quite.

The party proved to be the usual rout of noise and drinking and chat of people who knew each other very well, yet who were eager to entertain the leaven of strangers for whom the party had been given, by spreading a veritable red carpet of invitations and hospitality before them. Hope felt that Victoire must be gratified by Madenina's anxiety to bask at secondhand in the glory of the television coup which Craig had brought off for Belle Rose.

Watching Victoire with Craig, Hope tried to guess at the true relationship between them. But they gave away nothing. Victoire was herself, imperious and elegant as always; Craig was the urbane host to the party, never far from her, but slightly aloof, according her the attention she seemed to expect, but nothing discernibly warmer than that. Two people who, for their own reasons, wanted to keep their closeness secret might enjoy behaving just so in public, Hope thought jealously—wearing masks for masks' sake. Though why?

Her own vested interest was to find little comfort in Ian's curiosity and speculations on their way home. For Ian's view, based on no facts at all, he allowed, was that sooner or later Victoire and Craig would see the advantage of making a joint thing of Belle Rose's ownership and management. Victoire was widowed, Craig was

unmarried—what was to stop them? he enquired rhetori-
cally. To which Hope could only reply that there was
some gossip to that effect on the island, but that nobody
knew.

They talked about Crispin and Tina and the party,
and when he left her at the bungalow Ian's kiss was warm
with a feeling she could not share. She liked him. He
was companionable. But nothing within her stirred at
his touch. Her only response was a sense of gratitude for
his friendly homage, and if he thought himself in love
with her, he would not find that enough.

The next morning the television crew arrived in full
muster at the plantation. As a preliminary to their survey
of the estate Craig gathered them in the office for a briefing on the life cycle of sugar cane, its long history of use
by man and its importance in the markets of the world.

He told them he couldn't dictate their treatment of
the subject, but that he hoped they wouldn't neglect the
human approach—meaning the men and women and
children who had served and been served by cane over the
centuries; the families who lived by and for it now, and
the unborn thousands who would profit from it in the
future.

Listening, Hope experienced a recoil from her bitter
feelings of overnight. He wasn't all callous; he could
care, he did care for some things, for some people—for
those wives who had stormed the *boucan*, for old Eli
Caracas whom he had defended from Victoire, for all
his workers who answered his loyalty to them with their
own for him.

With all her heart now, Hope wanted not to think ill of
him, not to despise him for his treatment of Barbara. If

only, if only she knew the hows and the whys of it all! But who was to tell her, while Barbara kept her own counsel and he kept his? She had to suppose that only events—such as, perhaps, the announcement of his engagement to Victoire—would do so. And that was something she prayed she would not be long enough on Madenina to see.

CHAPTER EIGHT

AGAIN Tina had to await Victoire's pleasure before learning what her sentence was to be. Crispin had been sent home, fully recovered after three days in hospital, but now Victoire did not allow Tina to take him out alone. She was always policed by Doria, Victoire's housewoman, of whom Tina complained to Hope, 'I'm nothing but a chauffeur to her and Crispin. She sits in the car like a prison warder, and when we get out she walks a pace or two behind. She hardly ever speaks; I might as well try to communicate with a deaf-mute, and Madame never trusts me now with any errands she wants done—she always gives them to Doria or Crispin.'

Hope said, none too sympathetically, 'Well, you can hardly wonder that she's afraid you might desert Crispin again, can you?'

'As if I would!' Tina scorned.

'As if you'd dare, don't you mean? But that last time Luke Donat was as much to blame as you. Have you seen him since to tell him so?' Hope asked.

'Once.'

'And——?'

'It was only in the town, and we couldn't talk there. He'd heard about Crispin, of course, but he didn't make another date, and he hasn't since.'

'Do you want him to?'

'What do you think? I'm in love with him!' Tina declared.

135

'Even though it sounds as if he feels he's well out of it, and means to keep out?' As she saw Tina's face crumple to misery Hope softened. 'Look,' she began, 'I know what it feels like——'

'You don't. You can't! You've never been in love,' Tina accused.

(The Ice Maiden syndrome?) Hope said quietly, 'Maybe not, though I think I'd be cured of any man who played me along while it suited him, and then, when he had made trouble for me, didn't want to know.'

'*He* didn't make the trouble. It was just too bad that it happened,' Tina defended him.

'He knew you shouldn't leave Crispin alone, and he knew there was a manchineel on Cloud's Nest beach,' Hope maintained, and then pleaded, 'Tina love, it just isn't on. He isn't serious about you; he can't be. So if he does want to make another date with you, don't see him, will you? Nor try to make one with him?'

But Tina wasn't promising, and remained unconvinced. 'He can't mean to finish with me—just like that. We were both on our way somewhere and we only had a minute or two together. He'll ring me or write—or something,' she declared doggedly, and it was on that note of blind trust that Hope had to part from her.

Now spring was really on the march. Marked in the tropics by no lengthening of the daylight hours, nor by the new pale greenery of the English countryside, on lush Madenina, rainbow-coloured all the year round, it was signalled by the increasing strength of the sun, by the locals' quickened urge to celebrate every weekend with 'jump-ups' to the insistent clamour of steel bands, and the final readying of the canes for the first cut of the year.

Every estate took on casual labour for each *ratoon*, the arduous, dirty work of cutting being for the most part beneath the dignity of the permanent workers engaged on the regular husbandry and management of the crops. A few of these, attracted by the higher rates and bonuses for cane-cutting, would change to it for the season. But the daily queues at the Belle Rose office for vetting and despatch to the *boucan* for the issue of 'cards' were made up of men and a few brawny women who homed-in for the weeks of the *ratoon* and reckoned to live on their takings for as many weeks after it.

On Belle Rose this year matters were complicated by the television team's omnipresent cameras and trailing cables, and their insatiable quest for information on every aspect of the sugar industry and of island life which might promise 'good camera'.

It was on one such morning of hectic activity that Victoire's car drew up outside the office and Victoire arrived to demand that it be cleared of all the people milling in and about it, as she wished to speak to Craig in private. 'To you too,' she added imperiously to Hope. 'Please stay.'

'Mr Napier is down at the *boucan*,' Hope told her.

'Then have him fetched, please. I have a later appointment in the town and I can't wait.' With which Victoire turned to study the view from the window, registering an air of no-interest until Craig appeared in answer to Hope's message to him.

Then she told him, 'I phoned you, but you had already left. And as I needed to see Miss Redmond too, I came down.' She turned to include Hope in what she said next, which was, 'Tina is missing. She hasn't been back all night, and if for any silly reason she has taken refuge with you or your landlady *again*, I think I could at least expect you to have let me know.'

.For Hope, the effect was electric. An icy chill ran the length of her spine, and it was Craig who barked at Victoire, 'Missing? Since *last night*? And you've done nothing about it until now? Or have you? Rung the police or the hospital—no?'

'And advertised to the whole island that she has gone? You know the rate at which gossip runs here. Besides, I only learned she hadn't been home an hour ago when I got up, and Doria told me. And then naturally I concluded she was where she had run skulking before now— with your friend Mrs Paul and with her cousin here——'

'Which she isn't, of course?' Craig broke in to demand of Hope.

Hope said, 'Of course not. If she had come to us we'd have telephoned Madame de Faye and sent her back, as, I'd remind you, Madame, we have always done before. I haven't seen her for several days, and do I take it that last night you didn't know she was out?'

'Last night I knew,' Victoire corrected. 'I had given her the evening off after she had seen Crispin to bed. She wasn't entitled to it, but she had asked it as a special favour, though of course I no longer allow her to take the small car unless Doria is with her. So if she went out, she must have taken a taxi.'

'You know that she called one?' pressed Craig.

Victoire shrugged. 'I wasn't interested. As she obviously wanted to go out, she must have taken one.' With a glance at her watch, 'Well, now you know all *I* know, I must go. I have an appointment to keep.'

With his hand on the telephone Craig said, 'You'll wait, please, while I ring the police and the hospital.

When will you be at home again in case Tina turns up?'

Another shrug. 'After lunch some time. I can't say precisely.' But Victoire waited while he made the two calls, both without result—there had been no accident reported, no emergency admission. Whereupon she said, 'So now the police know, I've done all *I* can,' and was about to leave when Craig stopped her.

'Has Tina been seeing anything of young Donat since the Crispin affair?' he asked.

'How should I know? Barbara Paul had done nothing to find her an escort, so I introduced them. But knowing how I should react if she had seen him again while she still had charge of Crispin, she would be a little idiot if she had tried.'

'Girls who imagine themselves in love are apt to be idiotic by the standards of the rest of us,' Craig said grimly, and then, 'All right, I'll handle it. But try to be there, please, when Tina does go back.'

During their exchange they had both ignored Hope, listening, numbed with fear, but grateful to Craig for asking all that had to be asked and wringing answers from Victoire, however reluctantly she gave them. When she had gone he looked across at Hope, standing emptily, her lip caught between her teeth to still its quivering. He said, 'You're afraid, aren't you, that I could well have put it, "*If* Tina goes back"?'

She found her voice. 'Yes. That is—even if—if she's able to, she won't go back. She'll be too frightened, as she has always been before.'

'Yes, well—now we've got to trace her.' His hand went again to the receiver without lifting it. 'What do *you* know as to whether she has seen Donat again?'

Hope thought back. 'Just that they met once by chance,

and that she was counting on his making another date, but without, I think, really expecting him to.'

'Though by her asking for the evening off, it looks as if he may have done, doesn't it?'

Hope caught her breath, hating the implication of that. 'You're suggesting he did, and that she——? That he persuaded her——?'

'To spend the night with him? It's possible, yes.'

'But it's not! Tina isn't like that, however—besotted. She wouldn't, she wouldn't!'

'All right, though she spent the night somewhere, didn't she?' As Hope watched, he lifted the receiver. 'I'm ringing Planchet,' he explained, and waited.

When he spoke again it was evidently to a servant. 'Ah—busy, hm? Packing? Going to Europe at the week-end? Well, I still want to speak to him. So fetch him, please.'

A few minutes of silence. Then he was snapping questions one after another, and possibly for Hope's benefit, echoing the answers he got.

'So? You haven't seen her? You didn't make a date with her for last evening? So if she hasn't been back to our Great House all night, you don't know where she could be? But where used you to meet when you were seeing a lot of her?' A pause. Then—— 'No. "Around" and "At one of the beaches for a swim" won't do. *Where?*'

Again a pause before Craig's final threat of 'You'd better——' as he replaced the receiver and said to Hope, stating a fact, 'He's lying, of course.'

'That he hasn't dated Tina? How do you know?'

'He's frightened to his boot-heels—it comes through. But at least we have somewhere to begin looking.' He stood and crooked a beckoning finger. 'Come along. We're going there now.'

Hope didn't move. ' "We"? No, tell me, and I'll go. You can't leave. That queue, and there'll be more by now! And Ian Perse is coming to see you——'

'Would you allow me to judge first priorities for myself?' he returned sharply. 'If Donat is responsible for anything having happened to your silly cousin, I'm going to nail him for it, trip to Europe or no. Meanwhile Perse's business with me can wait.'

Gratefully Hope went with him after he had telephoned the *boucan* and rapped out some instructions to Winston Fortune. It wasn't until she was beside him in his car that she asked where he was taking her.

'To Witch Creek. It's where Donat admits they've been in the habit of meeting and going swimming.'

'But even if he's lying, and he did see her yesterday, they couldn't have spent the night there—on the beach!' Hope protested.

'There's a disused fisherman's hut on Witch Creek,' Craig reminded her. 'If Donat made a date with her for last evening and then didn't keep it, she may have waited indefinitely for him, and then couldn't get back.'

'Wherever she went, she took a taxi,' Hope pointed out. 'However long she waited, she could have come back in that.'

'We've only Victoire's assumption that she took one.'

Hope shook her head despairingly. 'She couldn't have walked out to Witch's Creek—it's much too far. She must have given up hope of Luke Donat's turning up after an hour or two at most, so she couldn't possibly still be there.'

Craig lifted a shoulder in half-agreement. 'Probably

not,' he said. 'But Witch Creek happens to be the only clue we have.'

Like Cloud's Nest, Witch Creek was a crescent of white sand, lapped by a lazy surf-line and sheltered from the rough coast road by windblown tamarisks and palms. Craig drew off the road in the shade of these, cut the engine and sat in silence for a moment or two.

Then, 'Coming with me, or would you prefer to stay here?' he asked.

Hope swallowed on the fear-induced lump in her throat. 'I'll come,' she said, and looking up, surprised an unexpected compassion in his eyes before he alighted and opened the car door on her side.

The beach hut was of rondavel type—round, beehive—thatched, it's walls of flimsy lattice, its rickety door permanently ajar. Hope and Tina had explored it once on a swimming trip together, and she was recalling Tina's coy giggle of 'Bet this is an "in" place for the local courting couples!' as Craig stepped to the door, forced it wide and then stood back to allow her through it before him. 'She *is* here,' he said.

And there indeed Tina was, sitting on one hip on a pile of the dried palm fronds which strewed the floor, supporting herself with one spread hand, the other protectively clasping her uppermost ankle. At sight of Craig and Hope she gasped, as did Hope, running to kneel by her. 'Tina—what?'

Tina winced. 'I can't walk,' she said in a thin high voice which threatened tears. 'I think I've sprained my ankle—look.' She lifted her hand to show her foot's purpling, angry puffing. 'And look——!' she whimpered, raising her face to the dappled light to show that it, as were her bare arms and legs, was tortured and blotched by mosquito bites.

Hope began in pity, 'Oh, poor——!' But Craig cut her short as he strode past her to lift Tina lightly and easily into his arms. When they returned to the car he ordered Hope, 'There's a rug in the boot; put it over her on the back seat.' And when Hope had obeyed, muffling Tina to her chin, and they were ready to set out, he turned in his seat to chide Tina with a wry humour which she actually answered with a watery smile, 'In future, *that* ought to teach you to sleep under a net, you silly young wench!'

That was all. No blame. No accusing questions. Instead, real concern and practical help. For people who could stand on their own feet—and Hope counted herself one—he had little sympathy to spare. But for the underprivileged, the unfortunate and the unhappy, he was a rock of defence. Which made his treatment of Barbara inexplicably out of character—didn't it?

On the drive Tina, embittered and disillusioned, volunteered her story.

Luke Donat had telephoned her to ask her to meet him at their usual rendezvous last evening. Desperate to see him, she had dared to ask Victoire for time off; unexpectedly had got it, and had taken a taxi for Witch Creek. Luke knew, she said, that she no longer had the use of a car, so she had dismissed the taxi at the beach, counting on his driving her home.

She had gone on foot down the beach to the hut. But close to it—'I heard—that is, I knew someone else must be there,' she recounted haltingly—'because there were voices and laughing. *Two* people laughing. And when I pushed the door and went in Luke was there—with a girl. One of the town girls. I don't know her name, but I've seen her about. And when they saw me, they laughed some more and Luke said, "Come on in. We've been expecting you——!"'

'"We"? Meaning himself and the girl?' questioned Hope.

'Yes, "we". And when I asked him what he meant and what she was doing there, he said that was the—the object of the exercise. That I should find her there with him, which should teach me, since nothing else seemed to, that he wasn't my exclusive property and that if I didn't relish sharing him with as many other pretty girls as he chose, then I knew what I could do about it, didn't I?'

'And you said?'

'I—I don't remember,' Tina choked. 'A lot, but I was half crying too. I was so *angry*. I know I told him I never wanted to see him again—ever. And he said, "Fine", and then to that girl, "Mission accomplished. Let's be on our way". And I let them go. I'd have *died* rather than go with them, but he didn't even ask me how I was getting back. They just—went.'

Hope drew a long breath of pity and despair, and looked at Craig, who asked Tina, 'And then?'

'I stayed for a long time, sort of—of *hating* him. Until it got really dark. Then I started to try to walk it, hoping someone might pick me up. But at the top of the beach I fell over some air-roots of the trees, and my ankle hurt so much that I hobbled back—just to rest it, I thought. But it swelled and swelled until I couldn't even stand on it. And then the mosquitoes began to bite, and the sand-flies, and—I think I slept a bit, but not much. And then it was morning, and I was still there, not knowing what

to do——' She broke off and sat up, thrusting back the
rug as Craig turned in at the plantation gates. 'No! *No!*'
she exclaimed in panic. '*Not* back to the House! I daren't
go back. Not there—*please!*'

Craig slowed the car. 'Where then?' he asked Hope.
'To Barbara's?'

Hope nodded. 'Barbara will welcome her, I'm sure,'
she said.

Events moved swiftly for Tina after that. Claiming hys-
terically that she hated Madenina and everyone, or
almost everyone, connected with it, she insisted on going
back to England; cabled her father to tell him so, and
snatched at the chance to travel by the same flight as Ian
Perse, who was being recalled temporarily to Head Office
for a conference.

Once, before she went, Craig called for her at the
bungalow to take her to Victoire, who claimed the satisfaction of formally dismissing her. Tina cringed, and
both Barbara and Hope protested. But Craig was ada-
mant that Tina must face Victoire, who had offered her
a job in good faith, and in leaving it without notice Tina
would put herself badly in the wrong.

'And of course Victoire must have her pound of flesh,'
Barbara remarked to Hope who, suspecting what she did
of Victoire, could not blame the bitterness in Barbara's
tone.

The following Wednesday Tina departed for England
with an air of shaking unwelcome dust from her feet. Ian
went too, but would be back for the Mardi Gras festival,
now less than a week away, which the television team
planned to film as a background of dramatic local colour
to their documentary on sugar. Meanwhile Luke Donat,

warned, managed to bring forward by several days his own flight to Europe. He had already gone, his return indefinite, Craig heard when he tried to reach him again.

'I should have known that rats run when they're cornered,' Craig commented to Hope. 'I ought to have taken him by the scruff of his miserable neck to Witch Creek; faced him with Tina and trounced him soundly in front of her. However, he's dependent on his father and Planchet for his keep. He'll have to come back, and I can wait.'

Already the mounting anticipation of carnival was in the air, marked by day-long 'jump-ups' which could last until midnight and beyond, taking their toll in an absenteeism which every estate had learned by custom to tolerate. As Winston Fortune expressed it to Hope's amusement, 'Things got to get worse before they better. Fat Tuesday, Ash Wednesday—they peak. But come dawn, first day cane-cutting, then rum done, fun done; man sober again, see sense and earn good cash.'

By contrast with the excesses promised for Ash Wednesday the festive turn-out on Shrove Tuesday was almost staid. The town was gay with bunting and street-stalls selling everything from paper hats and balloons and papier-mâché animated snakes and toads to samples of every kind of fruit in season. The highlight of the day was the afternoon parade of decorated floats and tableaux, an official, well-conducted affair with an early evening climax of speeches and prize-giving on the *savannah*, the wide park-like area at the town centre. Later most of the hotels were open to non-residents for gala dinners and cabarets, and it was only well after nightfall that preparations for Wednesday's daemonic activities were afoot.

Ian, returned from England the previous day, had invited Hope to dine at a luxury restaurant facing the *savannah*, and as the darkness deepened, they watched from its terrace the building of the gigantic funeral pyre to which Vaval, Madenina's traditional devil-spirit, would be consigned tomorrow night.

'Let's hope it will be a slightly more exciting affair than today's Parade. The team is grumbling that Torquay Regatta or the Lord Mayor's Show could offer them a lot more camera scope,' Ian remarked. 'They'll have my blood for suggesting they shoot it, if the whole thing fizzles out like a damp squib on Bonfire Night. And supposing it rains, as the rain here alone knows how, what then?'

'I'm told,' Hope laughed, 'that it could rain china elephants, let alone cats and dogs, for all the devotees of Vaval would notice. According to Barbara, they'll have been "jumping" and drinking most of the night, and from noon or earlier, the whole thing becomes a kind of tarantella frenzy, working itself up.'

'So I've heard too, and if the TV types are to be impressed, it had better. You'll let me come for you and bring you to it, won't you? We'll drive in and park, as we did today. I'll order a table here for dinner again, and afterwards we can stroll around and mingle, and see what goes on,' Ian arranged comfortably, as unaware as Hope of the chaos which a Vaval-pressured Mandeninan crowd could create.

To begin with, he had to abandon his car on an avenue at least half a kilometre from the *savannah*, for between it and this random parking every street and boulevard were jammed with people, most of them masked in black, many of them, the *diablesses*, the acolytes of

Vaval of both sexes, costumed in black-and-white, dancing in grotesque, curveting gyrations, and fêting Vaval on clarinets, trumpets and improvised steel drums to an insistent rhythm. Cha-cha ... cha-cha—on and on.

With his arm about Hope, Ian and she had no choice but to join and go along with the general direction of the crowd—an undulating snake of movement roughly towards the *savannah*. It took the best part of an hour to get there, and they never did achieve the refuge of the restaurant and their booked table. For the swarms which blocked its approach and filled its rooms and its balconies had already made nonsense of any reservations. The spirit of Vaval had taken over and was not to be defied.

Dusk was falling now. Time to light the pyre. The effigy of Vaval was ready to be thrown upon it. The *diablesses* were executing a wild abandoned dance around it. Ian and Hope stood, hemmed in by the shifting, pressing crowd about them.

'All right?' Ian mouthed against the racket of noise, and 'Fine', she mouthed back, surprised that she should feel so.

Normally she hated and dreaded crowds. But somehow she was excited and stimulated by this one in its frenzied expectation of the devil's doom to come. Guilty of mob hysteria? She supposed she must be, but tonight she was experiencing something of the same satisfaction she had had on sighting the green ray. Both that tradition and this primitive ritual were the island's own, and sharing them, she felt, gave her the right to fantasise that, however briefly, she 'belonged' to Madenina.

She thought about Craig, whose home it was, who belonged to it as she never would. Did he attend Vaval every year? Did Victoire? Or, having long outworn its attractions, had he perhaps driven her out of town somewhere to dine in sophisticated peace at some up-country luxury hotel?

Now the flames of the pyre were leaping high enough for the immolation of the effigy, and it was hurled by many hands, its grotesque limbs splayed wide. People shouted, mock-wept and groaned, '*Adieu*, Vaval! *Adieu*!' and swung hands with strangers.

Hope told herself, 'It's all very Fifth of November and Auld Lang Syne,' but for the moment it was more than either. It was her scene and she was part of it, and she reached for and took Ian's hand——

But it wasn't Ian's hand. It was the hand of someone whose touch and stature, masked though he was, she could never mistake—Craig, forcibly pressed so close to her side that she could feel the hard resistance of his thigh against hers. Ian was nowhere to be seen near by. The compelling drift and movement of the crowd must have swept him away. He couldn't be far off—— But this was Craig's hand she held; Craig, hooking a finger over his mask and pulling it down; Craig, thrusting and pushing her back through the crowd into a little pocket of space where he faced her, dropping her hand.

'What on earth are you doing in this mix-up, alone?' he demanded of her, shouting.

'I'm not alone,' she told him. 'I'm with Ian. We were booked to have dinner at Les Immortelles, but we couldn't get there, and we seem to have got separated. But only just. I thought he was still right next to me when he wasn't, and—and you were.'

'Fortunately.'

She smiled. 'Yes, but—I mean, I wasn't lost or really alone. In those few minutes Ian couldn't have moved far——'

'In which few minutes?'

'When they threw Vaval on to the fire. When I wasn't noticing much, but watching, and then wanting to do what everyone else was doing, and hold hands. But if you'll let me go back to where I was standing, Ian is sure to be there, looking for me and worried——'

'It's to be hoped so.' With a firm hand under her elbow Craig began to ease their way back through the crowd. But they had not progressed far, when suddenly he froze, staring, and she thought he must have spotted Ian.

But it was not Ian whom his free hand winkled out from the press of people about them. It was a young West Indian, drinking from a rum flask until Craig forced him forward, when he lowered the flask and stared back.

'So,' muttered Craig. 'You've come back. Where have you been—since?'

'Down Barbados.' The tone was sullen.

'All the time? And what as? Cane-cutter, eh?'

The man drew himself up. 'I, low cane-cutter? Waiter-man in good hotel, that's me.'

'Waiter-man—with paying sidelines. But you had a date with me, remember? Why didn't you keep it?'

A shrug. 'Not convenient that day, mister.'

'Nor the next? Nor any day since?'

Another shrug. 'No good, next day. Nor after. I go Barbados soon. Only now come back.'

'In time to keep that date with me—tonight. Yes, I know you'll miss the rest of the fun, but that's just too bad. You and I are going to have the talk we didn't have —then.'

The man brightened a little. 'You pay still, mister?'

Craig shook his head. 'Sorry to blight your hopes, my

friend. I never was going to pay you, and I'm not now. I just want to know why you *really* stood me up that other time, and you're going to tell me—or else. So come, get going while I deal with some other business first. March!'

It was so, Craig policing them both like a couple of escaped prisoners, that they eventually found Ian, to whom he handed Hope over with a nonchalant, 'Your property, I think,' as if she were a mislaid parcel.

Ian gave a long sigh of relief. 'Heavens, yes. I looked the other way for the wink of an eyelid. One minute she was there; the next, she wasn't, and I've been berserk with panic.'

'Well, neither were you there when I thought you were,' Hope pointed out. 'I looked round for you, but——'

'Well, thank goodness you found her,' Ian told Craig. 'I'll see she doesn't get detached again.' With which he tucked his arm into Hope's and clasped her hand. 'You with the fellows—the TV gang?' he asked Craig.

'No, I came alone,' Craig said.

'And——?' Ian looked an enquiry at his companion, who stood with bowed head, his hands limp at his sides, his sandals scuffing the trodden earth underfoot. Ian went on curiously, 'Who is he? You didn't find him bothering Hope, did you? If so, I'll——! Or is he one of your chaps from the estate?'

As Craig looked down at the man Hope had the impression that it was from more than his physically superior height. There was contempt in his glance. 'No,' he said. 'He wasn't making himself a nuisance to Hope, and I wouldn't employ him for free. It's just that, in a certain incomplete jigsaw puzzle, he's got to be the missing piece.'

CHAPTER NINE

BARBARA said, 'What was this man like?'

Surprised by the sharp urgency of the question, Hope stopped short in her account of the evening's happenings. 'Well, young,' she said. 'Probably belonging here, because Craig accused him of having come "back" from Barbados, where he said he had been since—well, since some occasion they both seemed agreed upon.'

'Yes, about that?' queried Barbara. 'You say Craig suddenly dived for him in the crowd—and what then?'

As accurately as she could remember it, Hope related the whole incident of Craig's capture and accusations, concluding, 'After we came up again with Ian, the man hardly spoke. He just stood there, looking resigned and sort of defeated, while Ian asked Craig who he was and what he'd done.'

'And did Craig tell Ian?'

'No. He said something cryptic, which neither Ian nor I understood and he didn't explain, about the man's being the missing piece in a puzzle, and he took him away.' Hope paused. 'Why, do you think you know him, and what Craig could have meant?'

Barbara did not answer at once. Then, 'I've an idea,' she admitted. 'But if Craig didn't say anything, I mustn't.'

'Do you think Craig may explain to you?' Hope asked.

'Possibly. Yes, I think he may, if he's right. If he is, it should clear up something which concerns us both. So yes, he's sure to tell me,' Barbara agreed.

'I'm glad, if it's going to help.' To Hope the moment seemed right to put a question she had long wanted to ask. She ventured, 'Look, Barbara, you must realise I've known how your relationship with Craig has changed since I came here. You were friends then, seeing each other often. What's happened? Why don't you now?'

Barbara shook her head. 'Of course you must have noticed. But——'

'But you don't want to talk about it?'

'No.'

'Nor even tell me the bare facts of what's happened between you? You may well say it's no affair of mine, but if there's anything I could do or say that might help, you must know I would?'

Barbara nodded agreement. 'I do know, and I do want to tell you. But I can't, without——'

'Without Craig's permission?' was Hope's shrewd guess, but Barbara's reaction was stubborn.

'I can't,' she reiterated. 'Just leave it at that, please.' Changing the subject, she went on, 'Go on about the rest of your evening. You and Ian stayed to see Vaval duly buried?'

For a moment Hope had been tempted to refuse to be deflected by telling Barbara what she knew or suspected about the source of that anonymous letter she had seen. But fearing another snub, she went on to describe the final cortège for Vaval around the dying funeral pyre; the waving torches, the simulated mourning and the massed chanting of a refrain in which the whole crowd had joined.

Barbara nodded. 'Yes, the *Chanson Doudou*—"*Adieu, Foulard. Adieu, Madras.*" It's the Madeninan version of the Madam Butterfly theme about a naval officer who has to leave his island sweetheart to sail with the morning tide. Nothing to do with Vaval, of course. But it's suitably sad and no Carnival ever ends without its being sung as a kind of bonus dirge for Vaval, whom everyone then promptly forgets until next year.'

As was expected, Mardi Gras exacted its toll of absenteeism from the plantations, but by the beginning of the next week plans for an unusually early *ratoon* were under way. Estimates of each day's probable 'cut' were made; the casual labour was alerted to show up at first light, and the designated areas were fired on the previous evening for the treble purpose of driving the canes' sucrose content up the stems, of clearing the undergrowth and of destroying or banishing any resident snakes or scorpions.

On Belle Rose, once the television cameras began to roll, there was considerable competition to be within range of their action. The cameras themselves were objects of much interest, the team subjected to much amateur advice. Everyone, from cane-cutters to cane-loaders, from the wives who carried water and picnic meals to their men to the hordes of school-dodging children, wanted to be 'in' on the final result. To satisfy the demand of everyone to see himself as the English screens would show him, still shots of each day's filming were put on show in the canteen, to the infinite jealousy of the other plantations and the vastly enhanced prestige of Belle Rose.

The harvest was going to be a good one, lasting several weeks. The television team, having got what it came for, was ready to leave at the end of ten days. Ian dated Hope for his last evening and took her to a restaurant in the town where they ate Creole food and danced to a steel band between courses.

On the way home he stopped his car on a quiet road, cut the engine and turned to her. 'We've got to talk, Hope,' he said.

'Have we?' He had been serious all evening, and now he sounded embarrassed. To put him at his ease she said lightly, 'I'm going to miss you when you've gone back. It's been fun, your being here, and you've been awfully good about taking me about.'

'Yes, well—you don't suppose I haven't enjoyed it too? Or that the prospect of seeing you again wasn't all the way behind my getting the Board to agree to send out the team? But——' he checked and wasn't looking at her as he went on, 'There's this, you see—I *did* want to come, I *did* want to see you and I'm going to hate going back. As for my being "good" to you, that's all hooey. Only—well, the truth is that if—if by showing how much I like you I've given you any—any ideas, then I've been terribly wrong. Because—Hope dear, try to understand this, can you?—I know I'm not ready to ask any girl, even you, to marry me yet.'

Hope was silent, knowing what it must have cost him to be so starkly honest. Utterly relieved herself that, for him as well as for her, their weeks of closeness had been no more than an extension of their earlier friendship, she said after a moment, 'Don't worry, Ian. I never did have "ideas" as you call them, beyond wanting to enjoy your company and hoping you enjoyed mine. And as I'm—I'm not thinking of marrying yet either, you can't think how easy you've made it for me to discuss it, supposing you'd wanted to, and I didn't!'

He kissed her then, quickly, lightly. 'Bless you,' he said. 'For not making me feel a heel. For liking me. For going along—It's my job, you see. It means so much to me, and I feel I must travel alone while I'm making it a success and until I can offer it to someone—you, perhaps, if I'm not too late?—as something I've *done*, not merely hoped to do. And that's why—well, if you're as much my friend as I know you are, you'll understand.'

She did. She had always known him as ambitious; that the people above him appreciated his value; that, as her uncle Lionel had prophesied, he would Go Far. Meanwhile she could only envy him for knowing himself so well. If only she could detach head from heart in just the same sane way—She reached for his hand and squeezed it. 'I've told you,' she said, 'I do understand. We're on the same beam, hm? And agreed that we're staying there?'

He smiled at her gratefully and started the car. 'Agreed,' he said. 'And bless you again.'

When they reached the bungalow another car—Craig's —stood outside, and when Ian took Hope to the door and parted from her with another light kiss, Craig was coming out. The two men exchanged nods and went together to their cars, leaving Hope to question—Craig, visiting Barbara again and at night? What had he to say to her after all this time of neglecting her? And had he known, Hope wondered, that she herself would be out, so that he would find Barbara alone?

That question was soon answered when she went into the house to find Barbara clearing wine-glasses and snack plates. Barbara said, 'Oh, you must have met Craig as he left. Soon after Ian called for you, he rang up and asked if he could come over, and he concluded you would be spending your last night with Ian.'

He hadn't wasted much time, thought Hope. She had left with Ian at least three hours ago. Feeling that as it had been she who had told Barbara about Craig's captured stranger, she was entitled to know more, she asked, 'You said you thought Craig would tell you about the man he caught on Vaval night—so did he?'

Barbara nodded. 'Yes. As I guessed, he was a waiter at one of the out-of-town hotels who had asked for an appointment to meet Nelson, my husband, and Craig at the flat Nelson and I had then. They hadn't a clue as to why he wanted to see them, and they never did learn, because he didn't turn up and afterwards he disappeared from the island completely.'

'To Barbados, he told Craig,' Hope prompted.

'Yes, and though Craig made enquiries at the hotel and all over town, there wasn't a trace of him.' Barbara paused. 'You see, it had to be Craig who asked about him because the day they had arranged to meet was the one that Nelson and Roland de Faye were lost at sea. Before he went, Nelson told Craig he wasn't going to waste a sailing trip just to hear what this man's business with them was; Craig could meet him alone instead. But though Craig waited at the flat with me for hours— until nearly midnight—the man didn't turn up. And then we heard about Nelson and Roland's being missing, you see.'

'Oh, my dear——!' Hope looked at the cruel irony of the story, and ventured, 'So that if Nelson *had* kept the appointment, he wouldn't have lost his life that night?'

Momentarily Barbara's lips twisted to bitterness. 'Nor would Roland. He couldn't handle that sized craft single-handed and anyway, Craig was so much better a sailor than either of them that if he had gone along that day, perhaps none of it need have happened. But it did.' With a gallant effort she squared her shoulders and managed a smile. 'And when it had, I daresay you can understand that looking for and finding this other man didn't seem at all that important, can't you?' she finished.

Admiring her courage, Hope said, 'Except that you could think, rightly, that he was the indirect cause of all your loss. Didn't Craig think that way? And does he know now why the man didn't show up? Or what he'd wanted to say to your husband and to him? I heard him threaten that he meant to find out.'

Barbara was stacking the nest-tables she and Craig had used. Not looking at Hope, 'Yes, Craig does know now. So do I,' she said, and stopped. Then, as if she regretted the implied snub of telling Hope no more, she added, 'I'm sorry, Hope. Craig knows, and he's told me. But we've got to leave it there. It concerns—someone else too much. Do you mind?' And when Hope shook her head, she made a conscious effort to change the subject.

'Meanwhile, listen—you know I've nearly finished work on my dictionary? Well, when I've corrected the last draft, Craig is going to send it for checking to a professor of etymology who's a friend of his, and then he'll help me to get it published, at first locally, and then further afield. What do you think of that?'

Hope said, 'I'm so glad for you. But you always did deserve whatever success it has. Did Craig promise you this tonight?'

'Yes. He'd always promised to help, but we settled the details tonight. We talked for a long time—more than we've been able to for ages—about all sorts of things. About Crispin, for one. Craig says Victoire isn't engaging another governess for him, which means the poor pet will be left more to himself than ever. We talked about you too,' Barbara added. 'Craig said he'd never known any girl quite as—well, "collected" was his word —as you.'

Hope's heart quickened its beat. 'Collected? What did he mean by that?'

'I asked him, and he said that if one took Tina as the most uncollected, featherbrained, teetering example in recent sight, and you as her opposite pole, that was what he meant. He said if you were warned you were about to step on a land-mine, he'd back you to go ahead without a downward glance.'

'Which I'd call foolhardy rather than collected, wouldn't you?' remarked Hope.

'That's what I said,' agreed Barbara. 'And that I doubted if you were really as cool as he thought. *I* knew you were warm-hearted, and understanding with Tina and altogether a dear. But he said the only time he'd ever seen you a bit vulnerably excited or eager was the night when you saw the green ray with him. Which reminds me—you've never told me that you did see it, have you?'

'No, I——'

'Why not? You must have known I'd be glad you had.'

Barbara's tone was more kind than accusing, and since she and Craig were evidently back on their old terms, whatever they were, Hope felt that Barbara could hardly be hurt by the truth she had shrunk from telling before. She said diffidently, 'I didn't tell you because of the foolish thing Craig did after I'd seen the ray. We were in his car at the time and—well, suddenly he kissed me—just like that!'

She watched a little smile come and go on Barbara's face. 'Kissed you? Why?' Barbara asked.

'He said you had to have a witness that you'd really seen the ray, and that the kiss was a kind of traditional thing which was always observed.'

'But it embarrassed you—coming from him?'

'Well, naturally. We—we've never been on those terms.'

'But after he explained that it didn't mean anything personal? You didn't mind then?'

'Not so much. I couldn't very well, if it really is the custom here. Which it is, isn't it? You should know,' Hope urged.

'And so should Craig,' Barbara pointed out.

'Then it was true? It was only a gimmick, as he said?'

There was a tiny pause. Then, 'Of course. Just an age-old bit of ritual which you needn't have resented at all,' Barbara confirmed, leaving Hope to the final abandonment of a vainly harboured wish—that 'the custom of the country' wasn't all which had prompted Craig; that he might have known a genuinely warm impulse to kiss her when he had.

Victoire had not allowed Crispin to visit Barbara again, and since Tina's departure the only news they had of him was through Craig, who said there were no plans for sending him back to school until after Easter. Meanwhile Hope knew that Craig often took him along when he had journeys to make by car, and one day he mentioned that he hadn't yet redeemed a promise he had made to Crispin to drive him to see his old friends, Victoire's former houseman and woman, Matthew-John and Sadie, who were now at the Montgaye estate.

'I have to see Lucien Montgaye on business,' Craig said. 'I shall be lunching there, so I'll take Crispin to spend the day, and if you'd care to come along too, you're welcome.'

It was his first offer to Hope of a whole uncommitted day off, and she accepted it as the unexpected bonus it was. He brought Crispin down with him to the office in the morning, and when he had dealt with his correspondence they set out, Hope sitting beside him, Crispin with the whole of the back seat on which to sprawl and bounce.

Montgaye, not far to the north as the crow flies, was a morning's journey by necessary detours around creeks, and tortuous skirtings of the lower mountain slopes. It was altogether strange country to Hope—the sugar plantations of the southern coastal plain left behind, giving place to jagged volcanic rock at the seaboard and tropical forest inland.

Monsieur and Madame Montgaye ran a cocoa estate, their home as unlike the Belle Rose Great House as could be. It was granite-built, low and squat, its thick walls a wonderfully cool insulation against the heat outside. Crispin raced at once to find Sadie and Matthew-John, while the Montgayes and their guests drank pre-luncheon swizzles in the shutter-darkened salon, while the men talked the business Craig had come to do.

Crispin claimed the privilege of eating in the kitchen quarters. The others lunched on iced calaloo—a crab soup; chicken steamed with rice and saffron and coconut ice-cream as pudding. The siesta hour which followed saw the men going out on a leisurely tour of the estate which Hope would have liked to join, if Madame Montgaye hadn't expected her to rest and take coffee under the giant immortelles which, Madame explained, were grown and nicknamed 'Mama Cocoa' for the protective shade they afforded to the crops.

Madame was a bright, friendly woman with a lively interest in her neighbours which she prompted Hope to satisfy.

She spoke compassionately about Barbara. How was she? A sad pity indeed that she had so withdrawn herself after Nelson Paul's death. She should marry again, *la pauvre*. But for that it was necessary for a girl to meet men, and whom did Barbara ever meet now but Craig who, if ever a man did, kept his matrimonial plans to himself.

... Unlike Victoire de Faye. Now that lady made *no* secrets of her intention to remain a widow no longer than it suited her! Not of course that she was in as powerful a position on that as might appear from her style of living. For it was said that she had inherited only Roland de Faye's personal fortune; that Belle Rose wasn't hers, but was entailed to Crispin, with Craig having all rights of the estate's administration until Crispin came of age. But perhaps Hope knew the truth of that?

Obviously Hope did not, and said so with an emphasis which, however, did nothing to check Madame's pursuit of her theme. Accepting Hope's hot denial of any knowledge of either Victoire's or Craig's private affairs, she said amiably, '*Alors*, no one knows the truth for certain. But there has always been a word said that there must have been some reason why Roland de Faye did not cut the entail in favour of his wife; in short, that where there is smoke there is fire, as they say, and that perhaps he had more reason to trust his friend to do the right thing by Crispin than he had to trust his second wife, who was only the child's *belle-mère*, after all.'

But for Hope this was too near the dangerous ground of gossip, and she was thankful for the diversion of Crispin's arrival in the garden, bringing such news as he had gleaned from the kitchen—of a litter of kittens, of Sadie's new dress which Matthew-John had bought her for Vaval, which she would not wear again until Easter, and of the immature cocoa bean which Matthew-John had cut open and given him the juicy seeds to suck.

Monsieur Montgaye and Craig came back and the party became a foursome again until, when the shadows began to lengthen, Craig said they must go.

Hope brought away with her a feeling of guilt. Yet how could she have stopped Madame's voluble tongue telling all she thought she knew, in the hope of learning more? Meanwhile, for all Hope tried to discount it, if it were true, her gossip had been shrewd. It gave Victoire the strongest possible motive for linking her future with Craig's, and it lent him the arrogant, possessive authority of his treatment of her. He was sure of her. He hadn't to make even a show of affection. He could befriend and kiss Barbara when it suited him and neglect her when it didn't. He could go around kissing—other girls—in the name of 'custom' and meaning nothing by it. He could want a robot for a workmate, despise her for being 'collected' when he got one, and engage himself to a callous vamp like Victoire for a wife. All this—she stole a furtive glance at his profile, praying that it needn't be—if the gossip were true.

The conversation was mostly with Crispin until he quietened and Hope's glance into the driving mirror showed her that he had fallen asleep. She signalled the fact to Craig by dropping her eyelids and a backward jerk of her head, and they were silent until they were driving through the streets of the town, when Crispin woke with a start.

'Crumbs!' He had clapped a hand to the pocket of his shirt and produced a bundle of four or five letters which he surveyed with dismay. 'Belle-mère asked Doria to post them, but she wasn't going out, so she gave them to me, and I forgot. So where can I do it now?'

'Just round the corner, on the Rue de la Vierge,' Craig told him. 'But wait, fellow,'—as Crispin was about to scramble out into the stream of traffic—'give them to Hope. I'll stop, and she'll post them for you.'

'O.K.' But as Crispin passed them forward Hope fumbled taking them and needed to shuffle them tidily when she had them. She looked down at them, then stiffened and still made no move to get out when Craig had rounded the corner and stopped the car.

'What?' he asked.

'This——' she said, heedless of all discretion, and showed him the top envelope of the small pile, addressed to Barbara in the same clumsy script as she had seen once before.

Craig took the envelope, scrutinised it, glanced back at Crispin who was absorbed in sorting the contents of another shirt-pocket, and abstracted it from the pile. 'All right,' he told Hope. 'Post the rest.'

When she returned to the car the letter was nowhere to be seen and he made no reference to it. He drove to the Great House and dropped Crispin there without going in, then on to the estate office where he took out the letter and threw it on his desk.

'The sight of that petrified you,' he said to Hope. 'Why?'

She flushed. 'I was utterly taken aback. It was so unexpected among Madame de Faye's correspondence.'

He was watching her closely. 'Unexpected? But not impossible that it should be there? You may even have thought you recognised it—or something like it? Am I right?'

'In a way,' she whispered.

'Then you knew Barbara has had a succession of these things. Who told you about them? Did she?'

'No. She's never mentioned them. Tina did.'

'Who'd heard of them from——?'

'From—Madame de Faye.'

'As one who should know—if anyone did,' Craig murmured significantly. 'But if all you knew of them was through hearsay from Tina, how come you jumped to what it was when you saw it tonight?'

'Because I found one by accident and had read it, though knowing I shouldn't. And because of a chance thing Crispin had said. About—about his stepmother's practising writing with her left hand.'

'Tell?' Craig invited.

She told him— the details of both happenings and of the intuition which had interlocked them in her mind.

'I couldn't believe it. I didn't *want* to believe it!' she pleaded.

'But have had it forced on you now?'

'I'm afraid so. It looks like it, doesn't it?'

He did not reply at once. He took up the envelope, slit it and scanned the paper it contained. 'If you've seen one, you've seen them all. I must say, anonymity does limit the writer's style,' he said with distaste. And then, after a pause, 'Would it help at all to know that I'd had my suspicions too?'

'*You* had? Of—of Madame de Faye?'

'Though without any proof I could take to Barbara.'

'She'd told you she was getting them?'

'After the first one, yes.' He replaced the sheet in the envelope and put it into his breast pocket. 'All right,' he told Hope. 'And thank you. I'll handle it now. May I drive you home?'

Bewildered, her mind a tangle of questions, she said, 'No, thank you. I have the scooter and I shall need it in the morning.' If only he were less non-committal! If only she dared ask him what this had done to his relations with Victoire! On her way to the door she turned. 'You are going to have to tell Barbara what we've learned, aren't you?' she said.

He nodded. 'Of course. If you haven't told her first.'

Surprised, 'You want me to? I may? Tonight, when I get back?'

'Surely? In fact, I wonder that, as her friend, you haven't already told her of your suspicions of Victoire.'

'I felt I hadn't the right. You must know why?' she hazarded.

But he didn't take up that gage. 'Well, you have the right now. To tell Barbara the truth with my blessing,' he said.

More puzzled than ever, Hope stared at him. He sounded completely careless of the effect of Barbara's being given the means to a strong case of libel against Victoire. Didn't he care then what happened to Victoire? *Wasn't* he perhaps as involved with her as Victoire hoped and as he seemed? And supposing he weren't, after all? Supposing——?

She was to have her answer without having to voice the empty, vain hope of that question when Craig spoke, putting a question of his own—'What would you say, if I told you I was thinking of asking Barbara to marry me?'

CHAPTER TEN

IT seemed to Hope that in the few seconds which followed she suffered a world of conflicting emotions, of which the uppermost were shock and a desolate ache of self-pity. Except for his occasional oblique praise of her and some rare overtures of kindness he had never given her the slightest hope that, should he reject Victoire, he had ever thought of herself as any other than the efficient robot he claimed he wanted her to be. For him, as a woman, she lit no spark.

And yet, and yet—her own feelings for him had needed to feed on *something*, and though her everyday sanity should have known better, it was not always the equal of the imaginary raptures of 'supposings' which the memory of one or two special moments could arouse.

Supposing, that first morning in the office, his hand intimately and unnecessarily on her shoulder *had* meant that he found her a little desirable? Supposing she had not been able to hide from him that in giving him her injured hand to bandage, she had been over-sensitive to the prospect of his touch? Supposing the deliberation of his kiss had been a genuine statement of a love which wanted answering? Supposing his arm about her for the purpose of that non-event of a snapshot had really been a lover's? Supposing—— But now, with the certainty which his question made clear, all the dreams exploded. Of course for him there was Barbara. However she might have misunderstood their differences and parting, there

must always have been Barbara. There was going to be
Barbara for him again. And she had to try to be glad.

Craig was waiting for her to speak, his look of enquiry
intent. She swallowed on a hardness in her throat and
managed, 'I—I'm awfully surprised. And of course,
happy for you both. I thought—That is, I——' She
couldn't go on.

Still watching her closely, Craig asked, 'Barbara hadn't
told you that when I stopped seeing her regularly, it
was she who sent me away?'

'No. She didn't say anything about it to me.'

'You weren't curious enough to ask?'

'I thought she would tell me, if she wanted me to know.
And when I told you I knew she was unhappy, you
snubbed me by saying there was nothing you could do to
help her.'

'Nor was there—then. The help she needed most at
that time was the truth about these letters, and about
that I knew no more than she did. And she had persuaded
me that the only way to kill the scandal which the letters
implied was being bandied was for us to stop seeing each
other. After Nelson's death she had rather gone into
hiding from her friends, and in order that the gossip
shouldn't have anything to feed on, she cut herself off
further from them. And for that alone, I mean to see
that Victoire shall answer.'

Hope said. 'She deserves it. But I thought—Tina
said that you and Victoire had an—an understanding.'

'On the subject of marriage? No way. I took her
measure a long time ago, and whatever ideas she may
have had about me, mine about her have never seen her
as a life partner.'

'And you've been in love with Barbara all along,' said

Hope, testing it aloud for how it sounded to her heart.

'I haven't asked her yet to marry me.'

'But she must know how you feel about her.'

'I think she does. But if you're as surprised as you claim, our relationship doesn't seem to have got through to you.'

'Only because of the break between you. And when Tina said you would probably marry Victoire if only for the sake of the estate, I was desperately sorry for Barbara, because I thought you'd thrown her over for Victoire, and I was sure, as I am now, that she loves you.'

'Though supposing when you learned I had no designs on Victoire's favours, I'd told you I had no intentions in Barbara's direction either?'

Missing the drift of his question, Hope queried, 'You mean—instead of telling me, as you have done, that you mean to ask Barbara to marry you?'

'Yes. Would you then have decided you must cast your matchmaking nets further afield?'

She flushed at the gibe. 'I wasn't matchmaking for you. How could I, when I don't know what other woman— or women—there may be in your world?'

'So you would just have been sorry for Barbara, and left it at that?'

'I suppose so.'

'And when I think the time is ripe for my proposing, you're going to be content to be glad for her?'

'I've told you—of course,' Hope said, achieving dignity at a cost which only her sore heart knew.

Except for the chatter of the tree-frogs in the darkening garden, there was silence on the verandah of the bungalow after Hope had recounted to Barbara the chance in a thousand which had delivered Victoire into their hands. But at last, on a long sigh, Barbara said, 'I suppose I should have known that no one in our set—or in the set Nelson and I used to move in—had as much reason to hate me as Victoire thought she had. But that she herself should actually dare to write the letters threatening me, I can still hardly believe.'

'But what grounds had she for hounding you as she did?' asked Hope. 'You've never told me.'

'No,' Barbara agreed. 'And I never understood it until we had most of the picture—or Craig had, when he picked up that man, Solomon Bain, on the night of Vaval, do you remember?'

At Hope's nod Barbara went on, 'And I told you about his having made a date with Nelson and Craig at our apartment?'

'But he didn't keep it,' Hope put in.

'No. But the truth which Craig has wrung out of him now is that he'd hoped to sell information to Roland through Craig about Victoire's having an affair with a French tycoon and about their meeting at the hotel where this man Bain was a waiter.'

'Was the story true?'

Barbara shook her head. 'We shall probably never know. But there must have been enough in it for Victoire to have feared what Bain might tell Roland. Because he's told Craig that she made it worth his while not to turn up for the appointment—which he didn't. But as I told you, Roland never had the chance to hear the story—he and Nelson died that day. But then Victoire, her own reputation saved, turned on me and on Craig, telling anyone who would listen and convincing herself too, I think, that Craig had "murdered" her husband by skulking with me at the flat, when his seamanship which was much better than Roland's or Nelson's, might have saved the boat. And then, when she was sure that Bain had earned his money and was well out of the way in Barbados, she found she had another weapon to her hand. Craig and I had cleverly got rid of my husband for the day, hadn't we? We were together in the flat until midnight, weren't we? Didn't even know about the accident until almost everyone else in the island had heard of it, did we? Which, except that we had planned it, was true. And though none of it was actually *said* to anyone who would admit having heard it, very, very subtly she let the doubt get around, and when the letters started, I was angry for myself and desperately afraid for Craig and Belle Rose. So I refused to let him visit me here again.'

'You suspected, I daresay, that Victoire would have liked to marry Craig?' asked Hope.

'Not until later. I couldn't believe she could forget Roland so soon. But as I knew she needed to strengthen her hold on Belle Rose, while I wasn't seeing anything of him, I even feared she might succeed.'

'Oh, surely not?' Hope protested. 'Except that you'd refused to see him, nothing had really changed between you and Craig. *You* couldn't have doubted him so.'

Barbara maintained, 'There were times when I could, and did. And even now the effect of all this leaking out could still be terrible for Belle Rose and for Crispin. Besides, Victoire will still be *there*.'

Hope said, 'I think you must leave Craig to strike some bargain which she'll be only too willing to keep. For instance, in return for her admitting to scandalising you and writing the letters, he'll probably promise that neither you nor he will make any public move against her.'

'She must lift her ban on Crispin's visiting me too,' said Barbara.

'I'm sure that will follow,' said Hope, and Barbara laughed suddenly, happily.

'Hope dear,' she chuckled, 'you can't know how good it's going to be, everything back to normal again. Crispin free to come here whenever he wants, and Craig around —as he used to be before all this happened—you can't *know*!'

But Hope could—of a friendship and a love which she had watched and envied and suffered with for months. She hadn't the right, without Craig's permission, to give Barbara a hint that she knew how things were between them and that he had confided to her that he meant to propose. But in spirit she could share with Barbara all that her marriage to Craig would have for its deep roots —the companionship, the seeking of advice, the arguing, the surprises—all that would go to make the happiness which she herself craved and would not know.

Aloud she told Barbara, 'I can guess.'

Now the last area of cane scheduled for harvesting had been fired, the crop cut, loaded, weighed and transported to the greedy maw of the mills. Belle Rose's bonus payments for a heavy harvest had been shared out, and celebratory jump-ups decimated the workforce while the money lasted and the revellers could still stand up and dance.

Hope, who all along had mentally set the end of the spring operation as the limit of her time on Madenina, found it upon her without her having made any move to train another secretary for Craig, or any suggestion from him that she do so. Suspecting that she would only act if her hand were forced, she wrote to her uncle for a ruling on the date he expected her return. Meanwhile she waited for the news either from Craig or from Barbara that his proposal had been made and accepted—a development which, oddly, in the week which had to elapse before she could look for a reply from England, did not come.

Bewildered and hurt that neither of them confided in her, she watched their association pick up its threads again. Craig came to lunch at the weekend, called in for drinks on one or two evenings, kissed Barbara heartily on greeting or parting from her, but either he hadn't actually proposed yet, or they were taking it for granted that Hope knew it was all settled between them. It was an inexplicable attitude, in face of which she took up a stubborn stand. She would *not* question Barbara; would *not* hint nor probe. They must keep their secrets if they wanted to. In any case, it would all be behind her soon. But that thought was less of a defiance than it was an ache which wouldn't go away.

Crispin came again to spend the day with Barbara— one of the terms which Craig reported he had imposed upon Victoire, as Hope had foreseen—and it was Crispin who first brought news that Victoire was leaving for Paris in the next few days.

This surprised even Barbara, though her comment of 'So soon?' showed that it was the timing, not the fact, that she was questioning.

Crispin said, 'She's nearly all packed and ready, and Sinbad and Doria and Dickon are leaving.'

Hope asked Barbara, 'You seemed to have expected this. Have you?'

'Craig thought it possible, in view of everything,'

Barbara said, adding to Crispin, 'What about you? Are you going to Europe too?'

Crispin shook his head. '*I'm* not leaving until I go back to school after Easter.'

'That's not yet,' Barbara pointed out. 'What's to happen to you until then?'

But that was a problem which Crispin was prepared to leave to the grown-ups. 'Belle-mère says Uncle Craig will do something about me,' he said complacently. 'Perhaps Sadie and Matthew-John will come back to look after me. I should like that.'

Craig, however, had other plans which he announced to Barbara when he called to take Crispin home that evening.

'Victoire has swung this on me pretty suddenly, with precious little concern for Crispin,' he said. 'And when I told her I thought I could persuade you to take him on, she said she might have expected that I could send him somewhere where he would be thoroughly and finally brainwashed against her.'

'H'm—polite of her. Remind me to set about a crash course in the brainwashing of minors, will you? Why this haste on her part to be up and away?' Barbara asked.

'I think it coincides with the imminent departure of a certain Monsieur Martineau,' said Craig.

'Martineau? *Martineau*?' Barbara turned to Hope. 'Yes, that was the big shot Soloman Bain claimed she was dating while her husband was alive. Remember— I told you? He left soon afterwards, but he's back again, is he?' she asked Craig, who nodded.

'On a regular trip, speculating in building land; leaving this week, my spies tell me, and as I imagine Victoire sees no future in letting a wealthy widower escape again, she's flying to Paris too.' Craig looked round for Crispin. 'Meanwhile, where's your protegé-to-be? It's time I took him home.'

'In the garden, teaching the cat to take a water-jump over a ditch he's dug. But the water won't stay in the ditch and the cat isn't co-operating. I'll fetch him,' said Barbara.

And still not a word, thought Hope, about the difference Victoire's final departure would make in their lives; of the relief for Barbara of not having the menace of Victoire overshadowing her marriage to Craig, as it had threatened her widowhood. Almost, that night, Hope broke her resolve to force Barbara—or Craig—into the open and demand to know why they were holding out on her. But her sore pride held her back.

On the day before Victoire departed for Europe Craig delivered Crispin to the bungalow, and on the next day Hope collected her uncle Lionel's letter from her post-box.

Its contents were much as she expected. It was indeed time now, her uncle said he felt, that she should broach again to Craig the subject of her training another secretary in her place. Since he had made no move in that direction, it seemed that he was fully satisfied with her. But the unwritten agreement was that her engagement had only been temporary, and while there was no need for undue haste, it would be rather nice if Hope could arrange to be home shortly after Easter.

There followed other news—that Tina had achieved a lightning engagement to a steady young man in Accounts and would be leaving the firm at Easter to collect her

trousseau and, with her mother's help, to furnish her new
house in Amersham; Ian Perse was to accompany the
Chairman of the company on a major publicity tour; the
film brought back by the television crew was apparently
a great success and would be shown on the nation's
screens in the early autumn. Lastly, Kathy Tremayne,
though an extremely efficient secretary, had become a
little drunk with power and was inclined to be bossy.
Uncle Lionel didn't know how she would take her de-
motion when Hope came back. But that was a bridge to
be crossed when they came to it.

So this was it! It meant that Hope's own crucial bridge
had to be crossed at once, and she felt sick at heart at the
prospect. And something of her depression must have
come through when she told Barbara about the edict, for
Barbara offered to break the news to Craig herself.

Hope thanked her, but refused. Craig would probably
be difficult, but that she had to face.

'Well, don't tell him baldly at the office,' Barbara suggested. 'Let me ask him to dinner on Sunday night; afterwards I'll make myself scarce, putting Crispin to bed,
and with Craig mellowed by a good meal and a punch or
two, you can tackle him then.'

But Hope insisted that it was an office affair and must
be dealt with in office hours. Craig would almost certainly make difficulties, but he would have to accept that
she must go. And anyway, she wasn't *afraid* of him. What
made Barbara think she was?

Throughout a restless night she was rehearsing the
interview. She would say this; Craig would reply that. He
would be obstructive. She would have to be firm. Firm?
Impersonal? Keeping her distance, as he would keep his?

While they talked, just a desk's width between them, and presently half the world——?

She decided to postpone the ordeal until the end of the day, so that after it they could part naturally for the night as usual. All she counted on was that they should be alone together in the office at going-home time, and they were. But the announcement which she had come to describe to herself as an ultimatum had about as much impact and explosion as a damp squib.

For to the news that she was expected back in England after Easter, and that between now and then she proposed to undertake the work she had come to do—the training of a secretary who would take her place, Craig said mildly, 'Yes, well, this was to be expected. Have you anyone in mind who could measure up to the job?'

This was a point which Hope hadn't expected to reach until after much argument, and perversely she felt almost cheated of a fight. She mentioned the senior clerk in the outer office. 'There's Nicola St John,' she said. 'What about her?'

'The one with her pigtails pinned to the top of her head, as if she were about to take a bath?'

'That's the one. She's going to night-school, learning book-keeping, and she's very keen to get on.'

'They all say that when one asks them what makes them think they can handle a job. What makes *you* think she's equal to it?'

Hope told her impressions of Nicola—that she was intelligent and adaptable and well-mannered—and looking Craig straight in the eye, added, 'She also qualifies in one respect which I believe you find essential.'

He looked interested. 'Indeed? And what's that?'

'She has a steady boy-friend, so I imagine she's proof

against the kind of infatuation against which you thought you had to warn me.'

'Without your needing warning, of course. But tell me, how long have you been storing up that one to throw at me?' Craig asked.

'I hadn't stored it up. It had just occurred to me as a facet of Nicola St John which I thought would appeal to you.'

'As it does,' he agreed equably. 'Astute of you to realise it. All right. In the morning, ask her to come to see me, and you can start work on her after that. I take it that you mean this as your notice to me?'

'Yes, please,' said Hope, signing a private doom with the words.

'I thought so, and I accept it.' He took a bunch of keys from his desktop and stood up. 'Meanwhile, just now I have a job for you which isn't strictly in your line of duty. Bring a notepad with you, will you? We're going up to the House.'

In his car on the way he explained that Victoire's houseman and woman had left that morning, but would be coming back to pack some things to be sent after her, working from a list which he proposed to dictate to Hope, and which he would leave for their guidance.

He unlocked the front door and led the way into the cool elegant hall. Dangling the keys from a forefinger, 'Have you ever seen over the whole house?' he asked.

'Just the drawing-room where you brought me to the party, and Crispin's little suite and the kitchen where the three of us had lunch,' said Hope.

'None of the rest down here? Nor the main rooms of the first floor? Well, this is the library——' he crossed the hall to open a door. 'And this, the main dining-salon, and this, a smaller one for family meals.' He waited while Hope looked round admiringly, touching the sheen of antique furniture and treading rich rugs and marble underfoot. They went side by side up the great curve of the main staircase and into and out of rooms aglow in the evening sunlight and finally into a long gallery, neither a living-room nor a bedroom, but a showplace for fine glass and tapestries and portraits, some of them dark with age.

Craig pointed to them. 'The de Fayes, male and female, from the seventeenth century on. This one, the first de Faye to own Belle Rose, and the builder of the house. This, his second son who inherited; his eldest died young of yellow fever. Crispin's great-great-great-grandfather, who married three times; and here, his grandfather and his mother, Roland's first wife. Roland himself isn't here. As you can see, the de Faye men postponed getting themselves painted until they were pretty rotund and showed off lace and leather and good cloth to advantage, and Roland didn't live to see that day. But they had their women painted while they were young and as beautiful as they were going to be.' As if in answer to a question Hope hadn't asked, he added, 'Victoire isn't here. She's made a special grievance of Roland's not having arranged it while he was alive, though I doubt if he would have been in a hurry, had he lived.'

'He wouldn't? Why not?' Hope asked.

'She was never the wife he deserved, and he had admitted his mistake before he died, which was why he gave me the guardianship of Crispin, whom she has always resented, and almost hated when she learned the contents of Roland's will.' Craig crossed to one of the deep windows. 'What do you think of the view from here? It's rather special, I've always thought.'

It was. It was possible to see the full extent of the gardens, the lawns ringed about by flowering shrubs, with terraced levels dropping down to a glimpse of water, an artificial pool, on the far bank of which a group of coconut palms made of their high fronds a filigree pattern against the sky. The backcloth to the scene was the dark mass of a small banana grove—the whole a study in greens and browns and colour, gently stirring at the impulse of the evening wind.

Standing beside Craig, Hope heard him saying, 'I don't think Victoire will come back this time.'

'Not come back?' Hope queried. 'Surely——?'

'No. I'd say the next thing we shall hear of her will be that she's marrying again.'

'But this is her house! She can't just abandon it!'

'It's not hers. It's Crispin's. The estate is entailed to him, and the house goes with it.' Craig paused. 'I suppose you're set upon going back to England when you leave the office? You wouldn't consider the job of caretaker here instead?'

'*Caretaker*? *Here*?' Hope wagged a finger downward towards the floor by way of emphasis. 'Caretaker of *this* house?'

'Well, perhaps in a French island, *chatelaine* sounds more elegant—no?'

'But the idea is absurd! I couldn't—how could I? You mean—keep it open for Crispin while he's away at school? But how could I possibly manage a house this size and of this elegance—alone?'

If it hadn't been for the seriously intent look on Craig's face she wouldn't have asked even so many questions;

she would have known he hadn't meant his own. But next he was saying, 'I wasn't suggesting you should take it on alone. In fact I propose to move in as locum tenens for Crispin myself.'

Hope moved her head bewilderedly from side to side. This was an impossible exchange—utterly cloud-cuckoo! She said faintly, '*You* propose to? Well then——?' and left it there.

'Well then?' he echoed in mimicry. 'Well then—what?'

'Well then—if you do that, you'll have Barbara. You mean you'll live here?'

'As Crispin's tenant, yes.'

'After you're married?'

'I'd hope to.'

'Married to Barbara? Then you couldn't need me around as caretaker or—or anything else.' She turned away abruptly. 'Let's go. I don't find any of this funny, I'm afraid. And I'm surprised that you should.'

Craig said, 'Then you can hold your surprise. For I don't.' He caught at her wrist and turned her roughly. 'I'm serious, Hope. I *am* going to live here, and I *do* need you here with me. You. Not Barbara, nor anyone else. You. Just *you*. Listen, I'm asking you to marry me, ice-girl mine. And if you find *that* funny, then——!'

She stared, wide-eyed. She wasn't hearing this, was she? From *Craig*—the aloof, the beloved out-of-reach, the not-for-her? She faltered, 'But this isn't fair. You're going to marry Barbara, and I'm—I mean, I've tried to be glad for you. When you told me, I——'

'But what did I tell you?' He had taken both her hands now and drew her close to him. 'If I remember, I asked you what you would say *if* I told you I had thoughts of proposing to Barbara.'

'Well?'

'But that was a trick question, my heart, designed to trap. And Barbara's idea, not mine.'

'You're saying'—Hope worked it out wonderingly —'that you weren't really meaning to ask her? Just——?'

'Just testing your reaction. When I told Barbara what I've come to feel for you, she said she'd already guessed, and that if I was afraid to chance my arm—as I have been—I'd be bound to find out whether you cared in return if I sprang it on you that proposing to her was in my mind. No girl, she said, could hide her shock if the news meant anything to her emotionally. We agreed I mustn't claim anything definite between us, or you would ask awkward questions later about what had happened to our romance. So we've kept you guessing, and all I asked you at that time was, What would you say if——? and waited for the result.'

'And—and what was the result?'

'I wasn't sure. Shock? You didn't appear to have flickered an eyelash, and within seconds you were wishing Barbara and me joy of each other. But there was still something—something in the way you seemed to "protest too much" when I pressed you. And somehow no spontaneity. If you were really glad, I'd have expected you to bubble a bit—wanting to know the hows and the whys, and asking about our plans. Instead, after saying in so many words that you were glad about it, you seemed to want to get it out of the way. And so, either A—you *were* genuinely glad. Or B—you possessed the poker-face of all time. I reported to Barbara that I couldn't decide which; she refused to believe that if you *were* shocked, you could have hidden it, and that if we kept you guessing for a while, sooner or later the questions you asked would—how do the politicians put it?—"declare your interest".'

'And you agreed?'

'Only to go along with her daft scheme while I chose my own time for asking you to marry me, confessing all this first, as I knew I would have to. And then what happens? I don't even get to choose my time. *You* force it on me by calmly giving in your notice! Upon which *I* had to do some deadpan face work while I thought fast and laid my plans to lure you here. To ask you—To beg of you—But I've told you what!'

For Hope, disbelief and a kind of precarious wonderment was gradually turning to an awed acceptance of the humble honesty of his pleading. Against all likelihood or apparent reason, he was offering her a sweet unlooked-for power with him; she could dare to believe he actually wanted of her all that she had to give. A little drunk with the heady knowledge, she ventured to tease him, 'What a lot of trouble we'd all have been saved, if only you'd questioned that second alternative of yours!'

His flecked eyes sparked and the 'dark' voice of her early mental picture of him said, 'You're telling me that if I had——?'

Teasing still, 'Who knows? After all, even Barbara couldn't guess the amount of training I've put in at not "flicking an eyelash" of emotion in your direction!'

He recoiled. 'You're throwing that in my face again!'

'You had underlined it. "You have been warned", you said.'

'I deserved to have my tongue cut out! But I was so tired of the starry-eyed hero-worshippers I seemed to collect and how could I have known how you were going to grow into my thoughts and my life with every day that passed? Didn't you realise how I resented that ladder-climbing executive type of yours? Obviously not, for you left it to Barbara to tell me that he'd gone back to England with his career Coming First with him. But I kissed you, didn't I? Didn't that tell you anything at the time?'

'Only that it was the custom of the country, after I'd seen the green ray.'

'And you believed me—of *that* kiss? Oh yes, I had the "custom" story ready, in case what I was trying to say to you didn't get through. When I thought it had—when you melted a little, seemed to want me ... like that; want me as I wanted you, I thought I needn't use the story and we could go on from there. But then you froze again——'

'I had to freeze; I dared not let myself think you were in earnest. There'd been nothing between us to let me hope you were.'

'And, fool that I was, I let you get away. But I did send you back to Barbara, knowing that she could blow my phoney bit of folk-lore out of the sky. Upon which, I kidded myself, you might be tempted to ask yourself why I'd really kissed you like that, and begin to be curious about the answer.'

'But I did believe I had to be kissed, as a kind of forfeit thing on seeing the ray. And that night I didn't tell Barbara I'd seen it with you.'

'Obviously, or she would have put you right. But why didn't you tell her?'

Hope admitted, 'A little, I think, because I wanted to hug to myself the memory of your kissing me; to—treasure it. And also because, though you weren't seeing Barbara any longer, I thought she was still in love with you, and that hearing you'd kissed me, even so trivially, might hurt her. And when I did tell her, after you'd come back to her, all she said about the kiss was that it was an age-old thing. Even then she didn't tell me the truth.'

Craig laughed. 'The devious wench! Though, come to think of it, if kissing isn't age-old, what is?' He bent to put his lips lightly upon Hope's. 'That's to be going on with—And Barbara has never been in love with me, you know. Nor I with her. She loved Nelson too much to be able to let any man take his place with her. In time she may be able to, but not yet. Meanwhile, she's picked up her threads alone, and she is content in her fashion. As for my loving her—no, except as a dear, dear friend. She has never had the other kind of magic for me, as you have.'

'You kiss her too.'

'Is that Demon Jealousy lifting its head? I trust it is. So yes, I do kiss Barbara; it says "Hello there" and "See you later" to her for me. It's a habit I got into before Nelson died, and afterwards I knew I mustn't stop giving her matey little kisses like that. She was going to be kissed so seldom in *any* way in future. Point clear?'

'Y—yes. Though one night she was in your arms, not just—matily. I was coming back from a walk after she'd asked me to leave you together, and I couldn't help seeing you.'

'Ah—the day she'd received the first of Victoire's billets-doux, and she was terrified about not involving me in scandal, if people were really making it. So she refused to see me again until they stopped, and that night she was breaking her heart for shame. I comforted her in the only way I knew. And you know the rest. How you began for me as a voice on a telephone, and then showed up as a kind of Galatea figure who refused to come alive to any invitation or even to a touch—Hope, your name? Well, let me tell you that you've been my despair for a lot too long, and what do you say to that?'

'I—don't know.' Gently Hope loosened her hands from his grasp and laid them on his breast. 'I'd rather show you,' she said.

'Ah——' He drew her closer, his hold an exquisite, breathtaking pain as his lips demanded the promise of hers. For Hope the world seemed to mist out hazily. Just now there were only Craig and her mounting need to convince him that she wanted him as he wanted her— with passion and delight and an awareness of giving and taking equally; totally sharing; nothing of herself too much to offer him, nothing of him too much to accept as his gift.

Their hungry, urgent kisses said it all, contenting them for the time being, knowing they had a whole future of fulfilment before them—the surges of desire, the quiet, everyday hours of companionship, even sometimes the stormy clash of wills, but always, always the sweet safety of belonging in marriage—the ultimate dependence of each upon each.

At last, on a long, reluctant breath, Craig held her off, though continuing to study her face, feature by feature, her body, line by line.

'No Galatea, thanks be,' he murmured. 'No ice-maiden, no robot. And mine, really mine? Since when?'

She searched her memory and told him—of the ache of envying Barbara, while still loving her for her cour-ageous self; of fears and fantasies which he was only too eager to match with his own doubts.

'I thought——'

'You put up a perfect smoke-screen——'

'I tried to hate you when I believed you'd deserted Barbara——'

'Tina told Victoire, who passed it on to me, that you and Perse had something going for each other——'

The sinking sun withdrew its golden light from the gallery while they talked. Close, elbow to elbow, they leaned on the windowsill, watching the world darken outside, as they discussed practicalities, made plans and looked ahead.

At one point Hope said lightly, 'I thought you brought me here to make an inventory for you?'

He laughed. 'Any excuse to get you here to myself and "show" you, as you put it.'

'And the list?'

'There never was any list to be made.'

'Just as there was never any green ray tradition?' she accused.

'Just as—— You'll find I'm a facile liar in the "All's fair in love and war" connection!' he said, and silenced her protests in a fully acceptable way.

Later he told her that Victoire had no right to anything but the money she inherited from Roland's will, but that he proposed to continue paying her a proportion of the income from the estate, as had been the arrangement since Roland's death. He had power of attorney for Crispin, as the owner of Belle Rose; Victoire had no wish to make a home for Crispin hence Craig's decision to move in to the Great House until Crispin was of age or at whatever later time he needed it for himself.

'Then you and I, my love, and any encumbrances we may have acquired, will have to move out,' Craig said.

'Where shall we go?'

'Perhaps I'll build you a willow-cabin.'

Hope giggled. 'A willow-cabin wouldn't stand up to your—I mean our—rains for long.'

'The sun would dry it out between times. Clay and wattle, then? Or shanty-town corrugated iron and flattened biscuit-tins? Or reinforced concrete? Take your pick——'

'I'm not fussy. I'd settle for a sand-castle with you, if I had to,' said Hope gaily.

'*With* a nursery wing?'

'If necessary——'

They laughed together and at a common impulse turned to go, taking with them in spirit the infinite faith of all lovers that of their future they had nothing to fear.